The Flag on
the Hilltop

"WHAT MADE YOU DESERT FROM THE ARMY?" (page 33)

The Flag on
the Hilltop

MARY TRACY EARLE

With an Introduction by

HERBERT K. RUSSELL

Southern Illinois University Press
Carbondale and Edwardsville

Library of Congress Cataloging-in-Publication Data

Earle, Mary Tracy, b. 1864.
        The flag on the hilltop / Mary Tracy Earle : with an introduction
    by Herbert K. Russell.
            p. cm.
        Reprint. Originally published: Boston : Houghton Mifflin, 1902.
        ISBN 0-8093-1517-3
        1. United States — History — Civil War, 1861–1865 — Fiction.
    2. Illinois — History — Civil War, 1861–1865 — Fiction. 3. Knights of
    the Golden Circle — Fiction. I. Title.
    PS3509.A63F5 1989
813'.4 — dc19   88-26469
                                                                CIP

CONTENTS

INTRODUCTION

Herbert K. Russell

Mary Tracy Earle occupies an unusual place among southern Illinois fiction writers: the descendent of a family that helped shape the region, she left her hometown of Cobden and made her way to New York City where she published two novels and saw her short stories printed in the best magazines of the day—including *The Saturday Evening Post, Harper's,* and *The Atlantic Monthly.* She succeeded so well at her craft that she is still identified in some literary histories as "a New York writer"—a phenomenon that may help to explain why she is not particularly well known in her native area.

This neglect is unfortunate. Mary Tracy Earle was one of the first southern Illinois writers to gain popular acceptance in the East, and she did so while frequently employing southern Illinois themes.

Born in Cobden on October 21, 1864, Mary Tracy Earle enjoyed the benefits of a wealthy and respected family. (Her father, Parker Earle, was a successful horticulturist and fruit farmer and the inventor [1879] of a refrigerated container used by the Illinois Central Railroad to ship perishable fruit.) In 1881, she left home and began her college education at the University of Illinois where she enrolled in a natural sciences curriculum and participated in oratory contests before graduating with a B.S. in 1885. She subsequently spent considerable time in the South before moving to New York in 1898.

She published her first significant short story in the June 1896 issue of *Scribner's Magazine,* and would publish more than forty others between then and 1904 when her literary production tapered off. Her output was never great. In some years she averaged only one published short story per year. Always, however, her emphasis was on characterization and quality rather than length. She paused to collect her stories on two occasions: *The Man Who*

Worked For Collister (1898); and *Through Old Rose Glasses and Other Stories* (1900). (The latter has two short stories with southern Illinois settings, each of them set in "North Pass," or Makanda; the former has three, in Cairo, Johnson County, and "North Pass.") She also published two novels, *The Wonderful Wheel* (1896) and *The Flag on the Hilltop* (1902). The former is a Deep South tale of small town life which has not stood up well to time; the latter is a southern Illinois regional classic — the best of its kind on the subject.

The Flag on the Hilltop is based on an actual series of incidents that occurred during the Civil War when Joshua Thompson's two sons (aged 18 and 20) scaled an immense tulip poplar tree on their father's hilltop farm between Makanda and Cobden and raised an American flag on what came to be known as Banner Hill. (The hill is three and one-half miles southeast of Makanda, or five miles from that town via the most direct road.)

Initially raised as a sign of support for the Northern cause, the flag was hoisted after Union victories on the battlefield, and it also stood as a reproach to a group of Southern supporters banded together as the Knights of the Golden Circle.

The Golden Circle was a secessionist civilian group that was well organized throughout the Midwest, especially Indiana, Ohio, and Illinois. At times it caused a great deal of mischief and not a few deaths. It was, for example, partially responsible for the famous Civil War riot in Charleston, Illinois, and for anti-draft movements elsewhere, and when not feuding openly with Union soldiers it created a great deal of tension through threats — the most popular of which was a never-to-be-realized plan to seize a Northern prisoner of war camp and free Southern soldiers.

The Circle was organized as a secret society and was said to maintain discipline through severe means, including death by torture for those who betrayed it. In extreme southern Illinois — in the Makanda-Cobden area — the Golden Circle's chief accomplishment was to offer aid and comfort to Northern Army deserters, which were numerous. Desertion rates from certain units originating in southern Illinois were extremely high (due to the region's political ambivalencies), and a good many native sons made their way back North and spent the war years hiding out in the hills near Makanda. In fact, the 109th Illinois Infantry, comprised principally of troops from Union County, was so depleted by desertion that its few remaining soldiers were eventually transferred to a new unit. Mary Tracy Earle acknowledges this historical phenomenon in chapter 4 of her novel when a member of the Golden Circle remarks that he has helped "many a man from the 109th that was tired of fightin' ag'in the South." Once at home, deserters relied on friends and relatives for food and shelter or on organized help from the Knights of the Golden Circle.

Membership in the Circle was high in the Makanda area (it was headquartered in bad weather in the Rendleman's Makanda hotel), with numerous meeting points in the hills and caves of what are now Giant City State Park and the Shawnee National Forest. Immediately south of Makanda, in Union County (where Joshua Thompson's two boys were raising their flag on the hilltop), the county's chief newspaper was openly secessionist, and 90 percent of the population was said to be pro-Southern.

One of those who knew just how risky such a flag raising might be was Mary Tracy Earle's father. In a letter to Illinois' Governor Yates, Parker Earle left this appraisal of the political climate in Union County on April 21, 1861, one week after the fall of Fort Sumter: "Union is perhaps the most intensively pro-slavery county in the State. Many of the most active and influential Democrats are heartily in sympathy with the rebel States . . . and would gladly seek their vengeance on such Republicans within their reach. Many of them swear that they will drive out every free Negro and 'Black Republican' from the county."

This is the historical milieu of Mary Tracy Earle's book and its two opposing forces, North and South. Although portions of the novel read like propaganda (at a key moment, two Yankees face down twenty of their Southern adversaries), the tensions depicted are accurate reflections of Civil War "life in a border country" — as one of the characters phrases it, and as Mr. Earle's letter seems to affirm.

The Flag on the Hilltop is interesting in its own right but has been made more so by the activities of four individuals who contributed to our understanding of it. The first of these is the most important.

After Mary Tracy Earle finished her manuscript for *The Flag on the Hilltop*, she first published it serially in the February and March 1899 issues of a magazine for boys called *The Youth's Companion*. News of her story made its way to southern Illinois where it came to the attention of Carbondale businessman Theodore W. Thompson. Thompson had a vested interest in the story, for it was he (along with his brother Albert) who had raised the flag on the hilltop nearly forty years before.

Thompson took note of the fictionalized account of the most dramatic moment of his youth in a turn-of-the-century publication entitled "Pioneer Days and Early Settlers in and around Makanda" (now in the possession of the Jackson County

[Illinois] Historical Society), and left this record of the raising of the flag:

> After the inauguration of Lincoln [in March 1861] brother Albert and I concluded to raise a large flag on what was known and called the lone tree, which stood on top of a very high hill on the great dividing ridge, between the waters of the Ohio and Mississippi Rivers, being the highest point of land in Southern Illinois, Bald Knob not excepted. Said tree was a tall tulip poplar between three and four feet in diameter at the trunk and some sixty feet to the first limbs. This noted tree could be seen in some directions fifteen or twenty miles away. It was quite an undertaking to climb to the top, and only five persons ever ascended to the top, viz: Charles and George Pelton, Lieut. William Sanders of Cottage Home, and brother Al and I. We first split from white oak timber four foot slats for rounds. After placing two spike nails in each round, we began to climb the tree by sitting

on the first round and holding to the body of
the tree with our feet, and with a hatchet to
cut away the thick bark and a rope to draw up
the next round, until we reached the first
limbs, and so proceeded to the tip. We sawed
off a small portion of the top and added a flag
staff some thirty-five feet in length, chained
and secured the bottom of the staff to the top
of the tree, and with a rope and pulley we
raised the stars and stripes, that could be
seen all over that section of the country, and
at that time known as the flag tree on the
hilltop.

The old homestead is now known as
Banner Hill, and is owned by my brother
Rolla. Here is where Mary Tracy Earle laid the
plot of her story "Flag on the Hilltop" that
recently appeared in *The Youth's Companion*.
This story interested every one who had lived
at Makanda during the Civil War. Many
families moved to distant states years ago,
but this story formed a connecting link for
their early life. They again recall the exciting

events of the early sixties. It was in the dark days of the Civil War that the Knights of the Golden Circle surrounded this tree to haul down the old flag, but from some cause their courage failed them. It was near the shadow of the old flag tree that the first meeting of the Union League was held. The old tree was killed by lightning about 1880 [1875], and has since disappeared, although another very large and tall poplar stands a little west of where the old flag tree stood that can be seen plainly from Carbondale, old DuQuoin, Bald Knob and the surrounding country.

Thompson's perception that the hill on his father's farm stood taller than its neighbors seems to have been clouded by the mists that frequently rise from the Makanda hills (for the ridge known as "Bald Knob" has an undeniably greater eminence), but in other respects Thompson's view of Makanda during the Civil War was excellent. He did not serve in the war due to severe rheumatism but instead spent much of the time in Makanda, where he farmed, and in St. Louis, where he was a hotel clerk, and in various Illinois towns, where he worked for the Illinois Central Railroad, his employer at war's end. Thompson remained in the Makanda area after the war, marrying and becoming a prosperous landowner and occasionally serving as host to notable figures of the day (such as the southern Illinois general and senator, John A. Logan, and others).

Thompson subsequently moved to the south edge of Carbondale (in 1887) where he came to own much of what is now the central campus of Southern Illinois University. His home stood where the SIU Student Center now stands, and he left as his legacy at least three place names significant to the town and the University—Thompson Street, Thompson Woods, and Thompson Point.

Theodore Thompson's youngest daughter, Mabel, also served to increase our understanding of *The Flag on the Hilltop,* for it was she to whom Thompson turned about 1903 to take down certain facts of his life as he narrated these from his deathbed. His narration, recorded in "The Wabash Notebook," now in the possession of the Jackson

County Historical Society, adds two important statements to Thompson's account of his wartime activities: he and his father Joshua — "Col. J. Thompson" — were active members of a local "Union League," a pro-Northern group that was the political opposite of the Knights of the Golden Circle; and Thompson the younger served part of the war as a Makanda-based bounty hunter of Northern deserters.

In the first paragraph recorded by Thompson's daughter, he tells of the Union League and of his relief when a party of Northern troops secured the Illinois Central Railroad bridge over the Big Muddy River (the railroad was the only direct link to the North); in the second he tells of capturing a particularly dangerous deserter named Woods:

> A part of a company of soldiers were dropped off at Big Muddy bridge to guard the bridge as it was a wooden structure. This gave the Union people (of S. Ill.) courage and they began to organize Union Leagues in opposi-

tion to the Knights of the Golden Circle.
Saturdays of each week was drill day. The
Government made a few arrests of the leading
copperheads which greatly discouraged the
Knights of the Golden Circle. The first Union
League in Jackson and Union counties was
organized at Col. J. Thompson's, my father's
house. The charter was issued by Geo. H.
Harlow Sec. of State. Alvan Robinson was
President of the Union League and myself
secretary. In holding our meetings we had
guards stationed out in military style. Many
Union and Southern sympathizers on each
side were waylaid and killed. In less than 2
years there were 19 killed in the vicinity of
Makanda and Cobden.

The country seemed to be full of deserters. The Government offered a reward of $30
each for their delivery to Cairo. . . . On account of rheumatism I could not enlist so I.N
Phillips of Cairo appointed me deputy Provost
Marshal to assist him in bringing in deserters
and to act as a detective. One of the worst

characters that I ever arrested was Bob Woods. . . . He had been arrested twice before I arrested him but had escaped both times from the guard house at Cairo. . . . I marched him down to Makanda and took him in a caboose to Cairo. . . . When we got there I put him in the guard house, got my voucher for $30.00, and returned home.

Further details about the life of Theodore Thompson are to be found in his obituary in the *Carbondale Free Press* for March 4, 1903; in John W. D. Wright's *A History of Early Carbondale, Illinois,* published by Southern Illinois University Press (1977); and in two fictionalized accounts, *Vinnie and the Flag-Tree* (1959) and *The Little Hellion* (1960), both by the daughter who compiled Thompson's deathbed narrative, Mabel Thompson Rauch.

A Carbondale contemporary of Thompson's, Professor George Hazen French, and Herrin newspaper editor-publisher, Hal Trovillion, also contributed to our general knowledge of Mary Tracy Earle's

The Flag on the Hilltop. French (1841–1935) served
as the State of Illinois' assistant entomologist
before coming to the University in 1878 to begin
thirty-nine years as a highly respected biology
professor and museum curator. He was familiar
with the novel and its locations and had at least
some knowledge of the identities of the individuals
on whom the heroes and villians were based.
Exactly where French got his information is unclear.
(Perhaps he acquired it on one of his rambles in the
country while collecting plant or insect specimens;
perhaps he simply left his University office one
evening and walked the 200 yards south to
Theodore Thompson's home and asked him.) In any
event, French came by a variety of facts about *The
Flag on the Hilltop.* At some point, he imparted
what he knew to editor Trovillion, who, in turn, left
the information with SIU's Special Collections Division in Morris Library. Members of the Thompson
family show up in one place or another as heroes of
the tale (as "Dr. Ford," and his nephew "Alec," and
friend "T.D."). Some of the others identified are
Knights of the Golden Circle. The French-Trovillion

notes are not without contradictions, but they are more useful than not, and form a direct paper link between the nineteenth-century protagonists of the story and later readers.

Hal Trovillion (1879–1966) had a full-time job as editor of *The Herrin Daily Journal,* but he too is important in this discussion, not only for the above association, but also because he liked *The Flag on the Hilltop* well enough to reprint it in 1930, noting as he did so that the book had been out of print "for some time" and that he wished to preserve "this pretty little story of a most interesting epoch." Trovillion was the owner-publisher of what was once the oldest private press in the United States and published a wide variety of authors on both sides of the Atlantic. He is also thought to be the "silent" source used by midwestern historian Paul Angle in his *Bloody Williamson* (Knopf, 1952), a unique history of small town lawlessness and Prohibition-era murder in Trovillion's town of Herrin and surrounding areas.

The object of this discussion, Mary Tracy Earle, spent only brief amounts of time in her native Midwest after the 1902 publication of *The Flag on the Hilltop*. In 1903, she received a master's degree from the University of Illinois and in 1904 went to Cuba (which had become an American protectorate following the Spanish-American War). There she served as a librarian and editorial assistant in the University of Illinois' agricultural experiment station, and it was there too that she met her husband, William Titus Horne, and married him on July 1, 1906. In 1909, she and Mr. Horne went to California, her home for much of the rest of her life. She published only a handful of short stories after her marriage, none of them a rival to her previous work.

Mary Tracy Earle revisited the area of her birth at least once, in the late 1930s or 1940s, when she was recognized for her literary work. She died, far from the Makanda hilltop whose history she had popularized, on September 7, 1955, in Riverside, California, at the age of 90.

Today, no banners fly on Banner Hill, although the hill itself is still a farm, and its elevation is still a boon to those who wish to send a message.

Orchards surround the hill, while at its top a silent metal tower transmits more messages in a minute than the Thompson boys ever dreamed of.

THE FLAG ON THE HILLTOP

CHAPTER I

IN WHICH A BOY GOING UPHILL MEETS SEVERAL PEOPLE COMING DOWN

THE shadow of a bridge across the railroad track darkened the car windows for a moment; the engine gave a long, frantic shriek, and the brakeman put his head in at the car door and called : —

"North Pass!"

It was in the spring of 1863, and nearly all the passengers on the south-bound train were soldiers who had been home on sickleave and were returning to the Union army. They glanced up indifferently, and then one of them sprang to his feet, exclaiming : —

"Looky yonder at the flag on the high

hill! Hurrah! Let's give three times three, boys, for the old flag!"

There was a rush for that side of the car, and the men leaned from the windows, waving their caps.   The train was rumbling into a tiny village encircled by green hills, and far away, from the crest of one of the hills, a glint of red and white flashed out against the sky.   "Hurrah!" the soldiers shouted. "Hurrah! Hurrah!"   The ringing of the engine bell was drowned by their cheering, and there was still one cheer to give after the train had stopped.

An exceedingly tall boy, with a face which looked oddly juvenile at the top of so much height, had darted across the car to look out of the window, but when he saw the flag, he drew back with a sudden darkening of his gray eyes, and towered aloof with an expression which might have been sinister if his face had been less young and round, and his limbs less coltish than they were.   As the train slowed up, he walked out to the car steps, where the conductor was standing.

" You said you would tell me, if you saw my uncle here to meet me," he said.

The conductor looked around the dingy platform. A few men were busy with trucks and packages, and a few idlers were exchanging jeers with the soldiers, not goodnaturedly, but with an undertone of unpleasantness on both sides. " No, Doc Ford's not here," he said; " I reckon he has other fish to fry than meeting boys. You won't have any trouble going out to his place, though, — that flag's on it, and you take the straight road east out of town."

" Thank you," the boy said, and running down the steps, he stood a moment to wave his cap with an awkward, sweeping bow of mockery toward the conductor and the soldiers, and then started along the road which led eastward out of the village.

When he had passed the last houses, he stopped on a little hill and looked around.

The village lay behind him, the houses showing through the trees like little white building-blocks dropped here and there by a childish hand ; on every side the hills swept away from him, range on range, until they grew faint and blue, and the sky stooped to kiss them.   There was something like welcome in the softness of the air, and the boy's face grew wistful for a moment ; then he looked toward the flag which was his landmark, and his expression changed as it had changed on the cars.

Just then the figure of a man on horseback came in sight on the crest of the next hill, and the boy started on.   As the two wayfarers approached each other, the man stared frankly at the boy, and when he was near enough said, " Howdy ? " after the friendly fashion which is heard only in the South or in places settled by Southern people.

The boy's face brightened.   " Howdy ? " he returned, with eagerness.   " Is this the road out to Doctor Ford's ? "

The man drew up his horse. "Yas," he answered, in his pleasant, drawling voice; "this-hyar 's the road out to the ole doc's. Are you-uns kin of his?"

"Yes," said the boy; "he 's my uncle. I 'm Alec Ford, but I don't know him; I 'm from Tennessee."

The man looked him up and down leisurely, and as the distance was long, he was slow about it. When he was done, he smiled. "You-uns did n't have no trouble getting through the army lines, did you?" he asked. "Looks like you could jus' step over 'em, if they did n't want to let you pass."

The boy colored a little, as if he were not quite used to being so tall, and were sensitive about it. "Oh, I have n't just come up from home," he explained. "My father put me in school in Massachusetts before the war broke out, and I 've been there ever since. Now I 'm ready to enter college, but I can't, for my father died last year and our place is all broken up, so I

have to come here to live with my uncle.
I've just come on the train and am going
out there."

"Doc had ought to have met you," the
man said. He spoke good-naturedly, but all
the while his eyes dwelt on Alec almost dis-
concertingly. They were exceedingly bright
blue eyes, and seemed to be the only things
about him which were not sunburned; for
his face and hands were sunburned very red,
and his hair was sunburned very white.

Alec frowned. " I reckon he did n't want
to trouble himself about meeting a Southerner," he answered bitterly.   " My father
always said uncle Mortimer had turned into
a Yankee."

"Sh-h!" said the man gently, "it's jus'
as well to be keerful about talkin'.   How do
you-uns know I'm not a Yankee myse'f?"

The boy laughed.   " You a Yankee!
Why, the minute you spoke I knew you were
a Southerner.   It sounded just like home."

" Well, that's where you-uns missed yore

"I'M ALEC FORD. . . . I'M FROM TENNESSEE"

guess, sonny," the man answered. "I was borned right hyar in Unity County, Illinois; but my folks was from Nawth Ca'liny, that's a fact, an' mos' all the folks round hyar is from the Ca'linies or Tennessy, or ole Kentuck', only there's a few Yankees an' abolitionists crep' in to spy on us. I'd jus' like to know how you-uns an' the ole doc is going to pull together; he's the ravingest, rabidest abolitionist in the gang. I expect he'll make you-uns play the spy on we-uns day an' night."

The boy's face flushed, and he squared back his shoulders, which usually drooped a little. "I'll not play the spy for my uncle or anybody else," he said. "I suppose, as long as I'm going to live with him, I can't do anything for my own side, but at least I won't do anything against it. I don't know what you mean, though. What is there to be done? There's never been any fighting here."

The man laughed and flicked his scraggy

horse with a twig he carried. "Jus' go 'long up to Doc Ford's, an' keep yore eyes open," he advised. "You-uns 'll see right soon if there 's anything to be done agin the South, an' if you ever git tired of seein' yore own country plotted ag'inst, an' want to git whar you can bear a hand for her, jus' skip out from the ole doc's an' ax yore way to Hiram Jeemes's. You 'll be welcome — kindly welcome — jus' bear that in mind."

Alec held out his hand impulsively. "I could n't leave my uncle and go to anybody else," he said, "but it 's very kind of you to say that, and I won't forget. Perhaps I can do you a good turn some time — I 'd like to."

The man's blue eyes danced. "Perhaps you can, sonny, perhaps you can," he laughed. "When you-uns has growed a little, maybe I 'll ax you to reach up an' pick off that-there flag that the doctor keeps a-flyin' in we-uns' face an' eyes; but all 's to be said now is 'mum.' It would n't he'p

yore growth none to tell the ole doc that
you-uns had been talking politics with
Hiram Jeemes."

"I understand," Alec said. "I 'll keep
my mouth shut. Good-by."

Jeemes's horse seemed to have fallen
asleep. He woke it by a jerk of the bridle,
said good-by, and rode leisurely down the
hill toward the village, while Alec swung off
up the hill, his mind whirling with new
thoughts. He knew that there were Confederate sympathizers all through the Union,
but he had not realized before that he was
coming into a regular border country. He
had supposed that everything north of Cairo
would be North, and everything south of it,
South, and although he had hated having to
stay in the North, away from the people and
the cause he loved, on some accounts it would
be simpler to be completely away from them
than to be here almost in the midst of them,
but under the protection of their enemy.

He wondered how much Jeemes meant

when he talked of plots and spies, and he tried to make up his mind in advance how far he ought to let his uncle's views stand between him and being of service to the South. His father had written once of the duty he would owe to his uncle if he were ever left to his uncle's care ; but just now the fact that Doctor Ford had not taken the trouble to meet him seemed to outweigh that letter of counsel, and he felt half inclined to turn and run after Hiram Jeemes, who had said he would be welcome ; it would be so much pleasanter to live with even the plainest people from the South than with a man who had forgotten his Southern birth.

But he plodded on, up one hill and down another along the sharply undulating road. Some of the hillsides were white or pink with blossoming orchards, and once in a while he had a glimpse of a house nestling among trees, but most of the country was still covered with forest, and stretched around him in every delicate yellow and gray-green tint of spring.

Often the road itself ran through forest, so that he could not see out, and in one of these sheltered parts it branched, one fork leading up to a gate, and the other disappearing among the trees. He thought the gate might open into his uncle's place, and he was wondering whether to go through it and see what he found, or to go on along the open road, when he heard some one whistling, and waited to get advice. Soon a little old man came in sight on the road inside the gate.

He had his hands in his pockets like a boy, and seemed to be looking up into the trees above his head; he was within hailing distance, but something in his brown, blank, hickory-nut face, all screwed up to a focus to help him whistle, amused the boy, and he thought he would keep quiet and see how long before the old man noticed him, and what he would do. But just before the old fellow reached the gate, he stopped, turned abruptly to one side of the road, and pulled

his right hand out of its pocket with a revolver in it, which he aimed at something
hidden from Alec by the trees.

"Hold up your hands or I'll shoot!" he
called.

Alec was through the gate in an instant,
eager to see what was going on.

"Hold up your hands and come out from
there," the old man repeated.

A figure moved slowly through the undergrowth out of the shadow of a ravine. "I'm
comin'," a voice said huskily; "don't shoot!"

The old man's revolver fell at his side.
"What are you doing here?" he asked.

The man in the woods came a little farther forward, and Alec saw that his face
was as white and thin as a dead man's.
His arms wavered as he held them above
his head, and his legs swayed under him
so that he stopped and caught at a little
tree. "Oh," he begged, as he stood beside
it, tottering, "you never used to be — hard
— on a fellow" — His legs yielded under

him, and when the old man and Alec reached him, he had fainted.

The old man stretched him head downward on the slope, and then looked at Alec keenly. "Who are you-uns?" he asked.

"I 'm Alec Ford. Doctor Ford is my uncle; I 'm going out to his house. Who is this man? Why were you going to shoot him?"

"Them 's Doc Ford's orders," the old fellow answered. "Them that can't explain theirse'ves hain't any business skulkin' in his woods. This-hyar 's a deserter from the army; that 's who he is, an' he 's come into the wrong woods."

"But you know him?" Alec insisted.

"Yes, worse luck to me, I know him," the old man growled. He looked at Alec steadfastly a moment. "See hyar, sonny, you-uns is from the South," he said, "an' maybe you would n't mind doing a good turn to a deserter from the Union army. How 's your talker, long or short?" He thrust out his own tongue to show what he meant.

"That depends," Alec answered prudently.

"Well, it 's this-a-way," said the old man. "When Doc Ford catches a deserter, he sends him right back to the army, an' it looks like this feller 's too sick to have his narves jarred on that-a-way. Now I know a place where he could be kep' quiet an' snug till he got a little better off. I 'm used to huntin', not hidin', deserters, an' it 's mighty queer work to think of hidin' one out on Doc Ford's place, but, sonny " — He stopped a moment; his face twitched and he looked away from Alec. "This-hyar 's my brother," he went on rapidly, "an' it 's God's truth, I hain't the heart to let the ole doc know he 's deserted. Doc would be good to him, an' cure him up all right, but, sonny, I 'd most ruther die than have the ole doc know how low he 's fell."

Alec forgot all his resolutions to be a neutral power.

" Oh, I think it would be better to hide him," he declared.

" Then help me carry him," the old man said, " an' we 'll take him to the Double-Barreled Cave."

They lifted the long, limp figure between them, and the old man led the way down the ravine. The undergrowth made the walking very hard, and it seemed to Alec that they took a long and devious route through the woods; finally he broke the silence.

" Do you live with my uncle Mortimer ? " he asked.

" Yes."

" What 's your name ? "

" T. D."

" Do you mean Teddy ? "

" Nope — T. D."

" Perhaps I 'd understand if you spelled it."

"You don't spell it, it's spelled a'ready. It's jus' T. D."

"Why, it's initials," said Alec. "What do they stand for?"

The owner of the initials gave a soft chuckle. "Mos'ly for T. D.," he declared. "They was for Thomas Deems when I was christened, but it looked like Thomas Deems was always too weighty for me, an' T. D. was jus' the right fit."

Alec asked no more questions, and they struggled on until they reached the sheer brown wall of a bluff and threaded along its base. Soon they came to a dry waterway opening between two rocks. They followed up its course, and where it broadened to make room for a round basin, in which a good deal of water still lingered, they laid the sick man down and bathed his face. He opened his eyes, and they gave him water to drink out of cupped leaves, but he said nothing, and his eyes followed them nervously.

" You need n't be skeered, Lafayette,"
said T. D. " We 're going to hide you in
the Double-Barreled Cave an' nuss you a
spell before we do anything else to you.
You ain't earned such luck, but it 's come
to you, so you jus' better thank the Lord.
Now, Alec, if you-uns 'll take hold ag'in."

Except for the opening through which
they had come, the high rock walls rose all
around the gap; but just across the pool
from the entrance, Alec noticed that the
wall was indented by two black shadows
one above the other, with a ledge of stone
running between. T. D. motioned toward
them.

" That 's the cave," he said. " The top
part is jus' a shallow hole in the rock; it
don't run back more 'n a rod, but we 've got
to climb up an' put him there, 'cause it 's
dry. The lower barrel runs back nobody
knows how far, an' it 's mighty damp.
Both of 'em 's wet enough after a rain;
then a spout of water comes down from the

top of the bluff an' there ain't no cave hyar,
— leastways not in sight, — jus' a stream
tearing down over the rocks, an' when the
sun shines out it looks like kingdom come
with a bow of promise shinin' acrost it.
But it would give a feller the rheumatics,
sure."

They carried their charge around the
pool, and then T. D. let him down again
with a contemptuous shake. "Lafayette,
you-uns got to get to yore feet now an' help
navigate yorese'f into yore hide-out," he
said. "Me an' Alec has been pack-horses
all right, but when it comes to climbin', we
ain't eszactly pack-goats." He gave an up-
ward jerk, the sick man came to his feet in
a bewildered way, and they half led, half
lifted him from one to another of the easy
foot and hand holds by which they climbed
to the upper chamber of the cave. The
afternoon sun had been shining into the little cavern, and the air was warm. Lafayette
dropped down exhausted on the rock floor

as soon as he reached it, but T. D. drew him farther back into the shadow, telling him to keep perfectly quiet until one of them could come back to him with something to eat and a blanket. Still he had not a word to say, but lay with his head buried in his arms.

Alec and T. D. hurried back through the woods, reaching the road at a point considerably beyond where they had left it. Just as they stepped out from the shelter of the trees, a tall man came in sight, walking swiftly down the hill. Alec looked apprehensively at T. D., guessing at once that this was Doctor Ford, but T. D. had screwed his face again into the likeness of a mildly disposed hickory - nut, and was whistling. The boy tried to compose his own awkward bearing into as serviceable an unconcern, but he was really very nervous, wondering how T. D. would explain their detour through the woods.

Of course his uncle would expect him to

be on the Southern side, and he had taken pleasure in thinking how emphatically he would declare his partisanship in the beginning, so that there would be no misunderstanding; he had never planned to hide anything from his uncle, or work against him in secret, and he did not like the feeling of it.

His uncle looked as his father had looked, too, except that he was older. The heavy hair pushed away from the forehead was white instead of black, but the intensely black eyes were almost the same.

"What was the matter, T. D. ?" the doctor called sharply. "Did you see anybody there in the woods ?"

CHAPTER II

"Did you see anybody in the woods?"
It was the very question Alec had been
dreading, and he felt himself growing em-
barrassingly red as his uncle looked him
over, waiting for T. D. to say something.

T. D. was slow and placid. "There ain't
nobody astir," he answered, with truth.
"We-uns jus' been over to the Double-Barreled Cave. I allowed as long as you-uns
wa'n't to home, I might as well interjuce
him to the place."

"Oh, all right," said the doctor. "How
are you, Alec? I was called at the last
minute to see a woman 'about to die,' so I
sent T. D. to meet you."

"An' T. D. was a right smart late," the

little old man interposed, " or else the train was a right smart ahead of time; I jus' stopped before startin' " —

The doctor shook his shoulders impatiently. " Train was ahead of time, of course ! " he declared. " Most everything 's ahead of your time, T. D." He turned to Alec. " Well, you 're here. I suppose you 'd rather be two hundred miles farther south."

" Yes, sir, I would," Alec said ; " then I 'd be at home."

" Tut ! " cried the doctor ; " you 're at home now. Your father and I never agreed about anything, and we always got along together by leaving each other alone. There were other people your father could have willed you to — your mother's relatives — if he 'd wanted, but he chose me because we respected each other. There are just two or three things you 've got to understand, and I 'll tell them to you right now and be done. Southern Illinois is a nest of copperheads, Confederate sympathizers you would call them. The truth is, the Ohio River ought to have run further north, and then this country would have been part of Kentucky, instead of being a rebel tag on the end of a Union State, — as full of secret traitors and treason as an egg is of meat.

" I make it my business to know what 's going on around me, return deserters to their regiments when it 's possible, and keep the government informed of the underhand movements against it. Sometimes my own movements would be of interest to the enemy, and you will be in a position to know things that the people round here — the people with whom you sympathize — would give their eye-teeth to find out, but I don't think I need to put your father's son upon his honor.

" I may not always explain my plans to you, but I shall not hide them. It 's not my way to hide what I do. I ran that flag up into the tree to tell my neighbors what to expect; it's in sight for twenty miles around, and those who wish to interfere with me or with it may take the consequences."

Alec listened, half in sympathy, half in defiance. He would have given anything to be able to answer his uncle's pride with pride, but he could only flush uncomfortably and answer, "I understand. I think you can trust my discretion, uncle Mortimer."

"Yes, I reckon I can," the doctor said. "Come on up to the house."

He led the way up the hill, and soon a little stone house came in sight, surrounded by a guard of forest trees. The world seemed to end behind the house, for the trees rose their full height against the sky. When they went indoors, Alec thought he had reached the most uncared-for place he had ever seen.

"T. D. is housekeeper," the doctor said laconically, and it was evident that T. D. was as much behind in the house as he had been about meeting the train. "I tell him he ought to build raised walks across the floor," the doctor went on, pointing to the untroubled depths of dust.

" An' so I will," said T. D., " when I git the time. I don't git much chance at housework these days — betwixt huntin' for Knights of the Golden Circle an' meetin' boys at trains."

" Alec," said the doctor, " do you know what Knights of the Golden Circle are ? "

" Why, as I understand it," Alec answered soberly, but with a gleam of fun in his eyes, " they are men of very good politics, who have formed a secret order " —

" Formed a secret order for stabbing the Union from inside," the doctor interrupted vehemently. " They encourage desertion, spy on the plans of the government " —

" An' meet where we-uns can't find 'em, which is wust of all," T. D. finished for him. " Are we going out ag'in to-night to hunt for 'em, doc, or shall we stay here an' entertain comp'ny ? "

"'Comp'ny' must look out for itself," answered Doctor Ford. "Make haste and get supper by sundown, if you can; I want to get an early start."

"Let me help, if there's anything I can do," said Alec, and followed T. D. to the kitchen. "Say, I'll have to take those things to your brother, then, shan't I?" he asked, when they were out of the doctor's hearing.

"Sonny," said T. D., looking up into the boy's round face, "there's nobody to take 'em if you-uns don't want to, but I don't know if I'd ought to let you. I would never have got you-uns into this scrape if it had n't ha' been " —

"That's all right," Alec declared impatiently. "We're in it now. What's the shortest way to get down to that cave from the house?"

T. D. told him how to go, and after supper was eaten and the two men had gone away through the twilight, Alec took the bundle which T. D. had prepared and went down a slope through a little peach orchard where the blossom-strung branches brushed against his face as he passed, and then along the top of the bluff, until he came to a place where he could climb down to the lower level at the foot of the rocks.

He was approaching the cave from the direction exactly opposite to that from which he had reached it before; but he had a good sense of locality, and only tried a few false gaps in the wall of rock before coming to the right one. He hurried around the pool and climbed to the upper chamber of the cave; it was already so nearly dark that he could see nothing as he entered it.

" Hello ! " he called, half aloud.

His voice came back to him, hollow and strange, as if he had called into a cistern, but there was no other answer. He spoke again a little louder, and the echo gained volume, but that was all. Then he went forward cautiously, expecting at every step to stumble against Lafayette fast asleep; but he found no one, and finally bumped his head against the low rock ceiling at the back.

He and T. D. had not gone in as far as that before, and unless Lafayette had crept still farther under shelter, he was not in the upper cave. Alec struck a match and bent forward, peering into every dim, black corner. He could see the floor and the ceiling meet all round the little cavern, and there was not a living thing in it except himself.

He climbed down, feeling quite dazed, and made his way for a few steps into the lower cave. He could not believe that Lafayette had gone far, because he had seemed too weak ; but perhaps he had crawled down to the pool for water, and then, feeling unable to go back to the upper barrel, had taken shelter below. As T. D. had said, the air was very damp, and Alec found the footing very rough. After slipping once or twice on small, round, water-worn stones, he lighted a match and looked about him, making up his mind that it was not worth while to search very far for a sick man in such a place.

There was evidently a small spring somewhere farther back in the cave, for a thread
of water wound along the stone floor, collecting here and there in tiny hollows. At times
the stream must have been large enough to
fill the whole cave bottom, for a thin ooze
of water deposit covered the half-dry stones.

A mark in this deposit caught Alec's eye,
and throwing away his burned-out match, he
lighted another and bent to look closely.
Something had slipped through it, just as his
foot had slipped on the stones behind him,
and the mark was fresh.

He hurried on, examining all the stones.
There were no regular footsteps, but here a
mark and there a mark, as if some one had
stumbled along, stepping as might be, now
in the water, and now on the slippery stones.
Alec went on until the passage narrowed and
grew too low to stand in ; then he found
his matches were all used. He called, at
first in a guarded voice, and afterward so
loudly that the whole cave clamored, but

there was no answer, and finally he turned back toward the glimmering twilight.

He was quite certain that Lafayette was hidden somewhere beyond in the passage, and he determined to go back to the house after a lantern and then find him; for he thought so sick a man might not have the strength to crawl out again, no matter why he had gone in.

Darkness was gathering fast when he returned with a lantern, and with some extra candles for it in his pockets. He held the lantern up and looked all around the rough tunnel as he went in. The rock walls were irregular, jutting out in rude forms which caught the light and sent black shadows flitting ahead of him. The walls closed in and down upon the passage so that he had soon to stoop and then to crawl, but after a while the tunnel enlarged into a series of chambers higher and larger than the space near the entrance of the cave.

He swung his lantern to right and left,

looking into every corner and cranny, and stooping to search for the footmarks, which led him farther and farther underground.

The cave was not beautiful, as he had hoped it would be. Its chambers were more like vaults or dungeons than like fairy pleasure houses. There was no white glitter of stalactites or stalagmites, hanging like icicles or mimicking the forms of animals or plants, but everywhere the sandstone walls were simple, dingy, and barren. Big, round boulders obstructed the way in places, and there were some jutting ledges and dark fissures in the dripping, earth-colored rocks, but nothing was brilliant or fantastic. It was a depressing place, in which it would seem more natural to find a man dead than alive.

Alec had no way of measuring time or distance, but he went on and on, until his whole quest began to seem dreamlike; he stopped short, realizing that for some time he had forgotten to search for footsteps, and had only looked around him with a mechanical interest in the conformation of the walls. Holding down his lantern, he saw that the trail on the floor had become almost continuous, as if Lafayette, growing too much exhausted to walk, had crept forward on his hands and knees. Alec found himself suddenly nervous, and shivering with cold and fright. It was horrible for any man as sick and weak as Lafayette had been to hide like that in such a place, and Alec dreaded to come upon him, believing that he should find him dead.

" Lafayette ! " he called timidly, and then was sorry he had spoken, his voice echoed so weirdly among the rocks.

There was no answer, and so, gathering his courage, he went on, and just around the next turning of the passage he came upon Lafayette, lying huddled against a wall which seemed to end the cave.

Alec held the lantern close to his face. It was even paler than before, and his eyes were so sunken that Alec was startled when

he opened them, shuddered, and closed them
again.

"I say," the boy began, forcing himself
to speak, "what made you come back here
and hide from us? We did n't mean you
any harm."

Lafayette looked at him again. "You-
uns was with T. D. ?" he asked faintly.

"Yes."

"An' T. D. sent you after me now?"

"He sent me with some stuff for you, and
when I could n't find you, I began to search
the cave. What was the use of your creep-
ing clear back here — the dampness is
enough to kill you."

"That 's what I 'lowed," said Lafayette.

Alec opened his candid gray eyes very
wide. "Oh, see here," he said, "I don't
believe anything of that sort. If you 're so
anxious to die, what made you desert from
the army ?"

The man hid his face on his arm, and his
voice came out muffled between his sleeve

and the rock. "I did n't desert," he said. "I went to sleep twicet on picket-duty, an' they drummed me out'n the army. God knows I tried to keep awake. I kep' studyin' 'bout T. D. an' the ole doc what raised me, an' right while I was proddin' myse'f awake I went to sleep. Twicet I did it, an' then they drummed me out."

Alec sat down on the stones beside him.

"Why did n't you tell T. D. ?" he asked. "He thought you had deserted, and that was why he wanted to hide you from uncle Mortimer."

"I aimed to tell him," Lafayette answered, "but when I seed him, I could n't get out the words. You-uns don't know T. D. an' Doc Ford. They 'd a heap ruther see a feller dead than know he 'd been put to shame. I did n't aim ever to come back to these parts, but I hid out in the swamp below Cairo till I got so sick it looked like I 'd got to get home. But when I got here, I could n't stand up an' name what had happened to me to T. D., an' so when I come to myse'f an' found he was a-hidin' me out ag'in, I jus' kep' my mouth shut an' waited for a chance to crawl off somewheres an' die. There ain't no good in livin' when you 've been put to shame."

Alec's eyes darkened in the way they had whenever he was excited. " It seems to me there 's a great deal more shame in being afraid to show yourself than there was in going to sleep," he said. " Maybe you were getting sick was the reason you fell asleep."

" Mebbe I was," Lafayette agreed indifferently, " but they drummed me out'n the army for it, an' I might better ha' died. That 's why I crept in here. I reckon my fever come up for a spell, too ; the cold felt mighty good."

" You 're cold enough now," Alec said, " and I 've got to get you out of here. What made you come in so far ? "

" I dunno ; mebbe my head was flighty,"

Lafayette explained, in his thin, flat voice. "I get flighty when the fever comes."

Alec stooped and passed an arm under him. "Now, try to get up and I'll help you walk," he said; but when he lifted, Lafayette slipped limply out of his grasp, too nearly fainting to be helped. Alec thought for a little while, and then remembered the bundle he was carrying, slung by a cord around his shoulder. He undid it, wrapped Lafayette in the blanket, and was trying to make him eat some of the food, when the candle in the lantern began to gutter and in a moment it went out.

"That's good," sighed Lafayette. "That-there light hurt my eyes."

"Then I won't light another just yet," Alec said. "But I'm going to stay awhile with you to see if eating doesn't make you strong enough to get out of here. If it doesn't, I'll go and bring T. D. as soon as he comes."

The sick man made no answer, and Alec

said nothing more, but sat by him, thinking of all the strange things that had happened since he reached North Pass. He could hear the soldiers cheering the flag again, and feel his own anger at the salute, and it was hard to believe that in so short a time he had not only pledged a sort of fidelity to the flag, but had entered something very much like secret service for a man who had failed in his duty toward it. He stretched his long legs nervously, and frowned in the darkness. Life in a border country seemed to be an exciting affair when one who was bound in honor to both sides was dropped into the thick of things as he had been.

The silence of the cave was so intense that he kept fancying that he heard sounds in it, and finally a sound came which was not a fancy, but grew plainer and plainer. It seemed to be the tread of feet, coming, not as he had come, but straight toward him out of the end wall of the cave. He thought that he must be deluded by an echo, and

that the people were really coming just as he
had come; probably the doctor and T. D.
had come home, and T. D., alarmed at not
finding him, had explained everything to the
doctor, and now they were hunting for him.

His first impulse was to call out to them,
but the fact that they did not call to him
restrained him, and he whispered to Lafayette
to keep quiet until they came.

The tramp of feet grew more and more
distinct, and there was a sound of some one
speaking, but, although the modulations of
the voice were quite plain, the words eluded
Alec; he seemed always on the point of
grasping them, but they always blurred away.
Only one thing was certain, the speaker was
neither his uncle nor T. D. There was an
instant of silence, and then a new voice
spoke, and he caught his uncle's name at
the end of a long harangue.

Then a shaft of light flashed on the wall
opposite him, moved along it for a little way,
and stopped. Alec started silently to his

feet, for the light came through a rift in what he had supposed to be the solid wall of the cave. He had noticed the hole while his lantern was still burning, but had thought it only an indentation. It was about on a level with his head, and looking through it he saw that it was a passage large enough for a man to crawl through, opening into a continuation of the cave.

The sound of footsteps and of voices was not echoed from the wall, but came through it from beyond, as if several men who had been much farther into the cave were now coming back.

If it had not been for Lafayette, Alec would have tried to creep into some crevice out of sight, until the party had come through the hole and passed by, but the sick man could not very well be hidden; so Alec stood his ground and waited to see what sort of greeting he would receive from the new-comers. Several of them were speaking at once, and their voices rose excitedly. At

last they came in view round a corner, and
the man who was carrying a torch stuck it
into a crevice in the wall; the others grouped
themselves in a circle, some leaning against
the walls, some sitting on the stones, and for
a moment they were silent, as if they had
entered a council-chamber and must now
weigh their words.

Those who had sat down were out of Alec's
range, but among those who were standing
he recognized Hiram Jeemes, the man he
had met in the afternoon, and it flashed into
his mind that this was a meeting of the
Knights of the Golden Circle, and that his
uncle would give almost anything to be
standing in his place.

"We've been soft-hearted long enough,"
a voice broke out. "What if he has stood
by us in sickness and death? That's no
reason for letting him thwart all our plans
when things of more importance than our
lives are at stake. If we were in the army,
we'd shoot down the most active man we

saw attacking us, and it's the same way here. The Lincoln government and the head of this military department are all rousing up to hunt for our leaders and our meetings, and it's through the information of just such men as Doc Ford. We've warned him already that he was interfering with us at his own peril, and now it's time to act!"

CHAPTER III

SECRET service was taking a form for which Alec was not prepared, and he needed time to think. He drew his face away from the opening through the rocks, for fear of being seen, but he might have saved himself the trouble, for the men beyond the partition in the cave were too intent upon one another and felt too completely secure in their retreat to be on the alert. Even in war time, when people hold consultations half a mile underground, they are not afraid that the walls have either eyes or ears.

A voice at once answered the speaker who had said that it was time to act against Doctor Ford. " I tell you," said this new man, " there are some lengths to which I am not prepared to go. Oh, yes, I know the vows I 've taken and the penalty of breaking them. Have n't I sworn in new members and held the ' shameful death' over their heads ? I 'm perfectly aware that any of you five, by reporting me at the temple, can turn the whole order against me as a renegade ; but you know very well that I 'm not any more a renegade than the rest of you are. The fact is this : We six control the organization in this township, and the township pretty much runs the county ; and it 's no use for us to get by ourselves to discuss policy unless we say what we think. You can turn against me if you want to " —

" Pshaw, now, Hutchins ! " expostulated a third voice, and Alec recognized the gentle, illiterate drawl of Hiram Jeemes ; " you-uns don't need to get so excited. It 's onderstood that what passes betwixt us six is betwixt us six. If you-uns get up an' says the same thing at the temple, it 's your own lookout ; but it won't get thar from us."

"What I want to have understood," said Hutchins, less excitedly, "is that nothing could be worse policy than to interfere with Doctor Ford. There are people here, our own people, that would rise right up if he was touched, to say nothing of the way that all the people who are too cowardly to take sides would get scared and call on the army for protection. No, sir, we can elude Doctor Ford, but we can't afford to fight him ; and what's more, if we could afford to, I wouldn't do it. There are some personal debts that can't be forgotten for the general good, and there's not a family in this county that doesn't owe some such to the doctor."

Some one brought his foot down on the stones with an impatient stamp. "Nobody wants to hurt him," said still another voice. "All that's needed is to raid his house, capture him an' T. D., an' put 'em where they can do no harm."

There was a laugh. "I'd like to see Doctor Ford captured without being hurt!"

somebody declared; "he'd fight like ten men. He'd sooner be taken dead than alive!"

"Either way would answer for us." Alec could not be sure whether the voice that said this was or was not the voice of the first speaker, but he was very sure that he would know it if he heard it again.

Then Hiram Jeemes spoke. "I 'lowed I'd let you-uns all free your minds," he said, "but 'pears like you don't come to much conclusion, so mebbe you'd like to know some news. Doc Ford's got a nephew come to live with him. I've seen the boy an' talked to him. He's a right pert youngster, an' he comes from Tennessy, an' hates Yankees."

"What's he here for, then?" some one asked.

"His father died, an' he had nowhar else to go," Jeemes explained; "but I tole him when he got wore out with seein' his own side plotted ag'inst, I'd be mighty proud to have him come an' stay with me. He 'lowed he would n't come, but hoped he could do me a favor some time, an' I 'lowed mebbe he could. He 's a mighty pert boy, an' the way I figure it, Doc Ford with a boy in the house to tell us what he 's up to will be a heap more use to us than Doc Ford hid out somewhar — ice-solated, so to speak, from the Yankee army an' government. What d' you-uns say ? Ain't that better than raidin' the ole doctor ? Thar ain't many of us a-honin' to lay our hands on Doc Ford. Some of us lacks the grit, an' some of us lacks the desire."

"Are you sure of the boy ? " asked the man who had wanted to take the doctor, dead or alive. "I 'm not willing to give up definite plans and trust to him unless I 'm sure of him. He may not have sense enough to be useful, and if he has, he 's not to be trusted until he 's sworn into the order."

"Looks like you-uns is mighty rushed for time, Kimmell," said Jeemes patiently.

"I 'lowed if he was n't skeered out of the track he 'd jus' foller his nose, without asking it whar it was goin', ontil it brought him in among us. 'Most every word he spoke showed how he was jus' a-honin' fer the South an' to mix hisse'f with his own sort of folks an' things ; an' I 'm hyar to say he 's goin' to be worth as much to us as a telegraph message from Abe Lincoln every mornin', tellin' us if he 's slep' well, an' what 's his plans fer the day."

"I 'm tired of all this," answered Kimmell. "Every time I propose a definite move against the one man who prevents our organization from being effective, there is some new excuse for postponing action. Why are we afraid to drill our companies at night, as they are doing in Indiana ? Just on account of Doctor Ford. And why have we never resisted the arrest of deserters when they 've been found ? It 's because that man is backed by the army, and never rests and can't be scared. I 'm tired of standing with my arms folded, and what I shall propose to-morrow night at the temple is a raid of about twenty men to capture Ford and T. D. and take them across into Kentucky, where there 'll be another party waiting to take them further. I say twenty men, because if the party is large, the doctor will be less likely to resist and get himself hurt. If he does resist, that 's his own affair."

" And I tell you," Hutchins broke out, as if he had been controlling himself from speech a long time, and could do so no longer, — " I tell you I will oppose that plan with every power I have. We all know that we 'll have to kill Ford before we can capture him, and it 's no use pretending that this is anything but a plan for murder."

" Very well," said Kimmell, " oppose the majority if you want to, but do it at your own risk."

There was a quick stir, as if some one sprang up suddenly, and then a general

movement and shuffling of feet.   Trusting
the excitement to keep any one from seeing
him, Alec looked through the hole again. At
first he could only see the back of a man who
was standing directly before the opening ;
then the man moved a little, and he saw
two others confronting each other.   Each
had a resolute face, one with red hair and
beard, and sharp, deep-set blue eyes ; the
other very dark, with a skin so tanned that
it looked as coppery as an Indian's, in the
rich torchlight.

The boy stared from one to the other,
baffled in his attempt to tell which it was
who was willing to risk his life for an enemy,
and which believed that to consider his personal obligation would be treason to his
cause.   Jeemes stood a little to one side,
blinking at them from behind his torch as
if he were amused.

" Pshaw, now, boys," he drawled ; " looks
like we-uns cain't never be of one mind.
Let 's go home an' sleep on this hyar riddle

before decidin' how we 'll answer it to-morrow night. Only be sure you recollec' that thar peart, long-legged boy in yore dreams. He 's too good a keerd to be shoved in between trays an' deuces out o' sight."

"Hiram 's right," said other voices. "Let 's go home."

Hutchins and Kimmell relaxed from their defiant attitudes, and Jeemes picked up the torch. Alec drew back again, his heart pounding against his ribs. "Get up!" he whispered to Lafayette; "get up! They 're coming, and we 've got to hide in some crack or they 'll know we 've heard. I want time to think more before I know what to do. They 'll be crawling through the hole and jumping down on you in a minute. Put your arms around my neck."

He grasped Lafayette, blanket and all, and was staggering to his feet with him, when the torchlight began to recede along the wall instead of flashing brighter through the hole. "What in the world!" he muttered, and letting Lafayette to the ground again, crouched listening. There was a sound of footsteps, and a few more words among the men, and the light continued to recede until it left the wall.

He sprang back to the hole, and clambering up and into it, stared after the retreating light. He could see all of the council-room now. It was a long, low, rocky chamber, like many which he had passed through ; the men had reached the farther end of it, and just as Alec caught sight of them, Jeemes passed around a corner with the torch. The light still shone back obliquely on the others as they followed him, until one by one they turned the corner and were lost to view. Then the light edged slowly along the wall until finally the torch-bearer rounded some new corner beyond, and it vanished suddenly, leaving Alec in darkness for a second time.

He drew himself through the hole and dropped down on the other side, determined to follow until he found out why they went farther and farther underground instead of starting toward the mouth of the cave. He was too much surprised to have even a conjecture about it, but he meant to know, and he ran through the open space which he had seen, hoping to catch up with the last glimmer from the torch and have it to guide him through the unfamiliar passages beyond. But in his hurry his foot slipped, and he fell at full length on the floor with a loud sound.

The blow to his head confused him a little, and he lay quite still and waited to see what would happen next. The men came running back and found him outspread on the floor of the council-room, as if he had fallen from the roof; he lifted his head and stared at them with interest, and they stared openmouthed at him.

Jeemes was the first to speak. "Sonny," he began, in a mildly curious tone, "would you-uns mind tellin' us whar you 've drapped from, an' what you 're doin' hyar? 'Pears

to me the ole doctor has set you to playin'
spy on we-uns pretty soon."

Alec lifted himself on his elbow. "I'm
not a spy," he said. "I belong to the South,
but I'm not a spy, either for my enemies or
my friends." And then, with the men press-
ing close around him, each asking a different
question and claiming his answer first, he
told the story of his meeting with T. D. and
Lafayette, and all that followed, up to his
fall. Fortunately he knew nothing more of
his uncle's plans than the whole country
knew, so there was nothing which he was
bound in honor to conceal.

After the first outburst of excitement, the
men listened intently, only interrupting him
with a few keen questions. Their faces were
set and eager, in a circle round him, and when
he described the Double-Barreled Cave and
the way in which he had followed the foot-
prints farther and farther until he found
Lafayette lying by the rock wall which ap-
parently ended the cave, they exchanged

glances of bewilderment which changed into surprised comprehension when he pointed to the hole through which he had crept to follow them.

Hiram Jeemes nearly burst out with an exclamation, but Kimmell, who proved to be the red-haired man, motioned to him to be still, and spoke to Alec himself.

"I believe you 've told us a straight story," he said, "but whether you come to spy or not, you 've heard more than I 'll trust you to take back and keep to yourself. You belong to the South now, sure enough, and we 'll take you along for safe-keeping; you 'll be in the hands of friends instead of enemies, that 's all."

"Yes," said several of the other men, "that 's the best thing that can be done."

"An' Lafayette," said Hiram Jeemes. "We-uns had n't ought to ferget that Lafayette is in this deal."

"Take him along," said Kimmell. "Wipe the slate clean."

Kimmell climbed up and through the hole; Jeemes passed him the torch, and several of the men followed, Alec among them. They found Lafayette lying just as Alec had found him; but this time he did not open his eyes when the light fell on him. Alec knelt down and spoke to him, but he did not answer. Then Kimmell shook him, but the thin figure settled limply upon the stones when it was released. Kimmell felt above his heart and found it beating very faintly. " I don't believe he 'll live an hour," he said, " and yet I don't dare leave him. Help me to boost him up, boys; we 'll have hard work putting him through that hole."

Alec turned to a man beside him. " Why do you carry a sick man like that any farther into the cave? " he asked. " If you 're going to take him away with you, why don't you take him straight out and be done? "

" That 's just what we aim to do," the man answered. " Hain't you caught the idea yet that there 's two mouths to this-here cave?

Nobody ever guessed it until you crawled through that hole. We did n't come in by way of Doctor Ford's. I did n't know myself that there was a cave on his place. We came in from the other side of the hill through a cave called the Devil's Den. It 's on Hiram Jeemes's farm, an' now you 've showed us that the two caves are all one tunnel under the hill. My kingdom, but if Ford had a-knowed it, would n't he have kept the road hot under here ! "

Alec rubbed his forehead. " Oh," he said, and then kept silent while the men worked patiently and gently over Lafayette. One of those on the other side of the wall had to climb into the hole, reach down for him, and draw him through. He neither spoke nor stirred, and seemed entirely unconscious of what was going on, but once, when they were all on the other side, and the torchlight chanced to fall sharply into his face again, Alec saw his eyelids quiver for an instant, as if the brightness troubled them.

Four of the men carried him in his blanket, Jeemes walked ahead with the torch, and Kimmell followed with Alec. The cave was roomier and rather less damp on this side of the partition, but the winding passages and desolate-looking chambers were much the same.

After they had been walking quite a long time, Jeemes turned round, signaled to them, and then extinguished the torch. They were within a few yards of the cave mouth, and the next turning would have brought their light in view from outside; but the men were accustomed to the way, and walked on almost as if they could see. At last Alec looked up and saw the stars above him. The outer air felt dry and sweet upon his face, and the dim country stretched around him in great, dark, obscure masses which he knew were woods and fields.

They followed a path through a bit of woodland, at the edge of which there was a halt while Jeemes let down a rail fence, so

that the men who were carrying Lafayette
would not have to climb it.   Kimmell and
Alec put it up after the bearers had passed,
and then followed on, now going through an
orchard where the night air was densely
sweet, and then across a ploughed field smell-
ing of fresh earth.

Another fence was let down and put up
again, they passed through another bit of
woods, and came out beside a barnyard and
a low log stable.   Beyond this a house could
just be discerned on a little knoll.   Jeemes
hurried forward, and in a moment a woman's
voice called out to him guardedly.   He answered ; then a light shone from the house,
and as Alec came up he saw that it was
one of those double log cabins, linked by an
open passageway, such as the Southwestern
pioneers so often built.   Like everything
connected with Hiram Jeemes, it made him
think of Tennessee.

Jeemes told him to go inside, and he found
himself in the room where the light was.

There were two beds in it, and three white-headed children were asleep in one of them. A ladder in one corner led up to an opening in the low loft. The men outside consulted hurriedly, then brought Lafayette in and carried him up the ladder. Alec followed.

" Are we to stay here ? " he asked.

" He is," Kimmell answered, " because he 's too sick to carry any further. If he gets well, you may see him where you 're going."

" Is that far ? "

" Depends on how you reckon distance. Jeemes is harnessing up his team to take you, and a few of us will go along to see you safe. It 's a brother of Jeemes's we 're going to take you to. You 'll be well treated if you don't try to get away, and I don't see why you should."

" I wish I could stay with Lafayette," Alec said.

" Mrs. Jeemes is a good nurse," Kimmell answered reassuringly ; " she 'll do more for him than you could, so you need n't worry. She 's starting a fire to heat blankets and stones for his feet now. You can stay by him, though, until the team is ready."

Alec knelt and began rubbing the sick man's thin, cold hands. The other men went down the ladder, and the moment they were gone Lafayette opened his eyes. " Sh-h," he breathed, " I 've knowed what was goin' on. 'T wa'n't no good fer me to talk, an' so I jus' kep' still an' limber." His weak whisper sank almost too low to be heard. " Keepin' limber 's a mighty good thing — when you cain't do nothin' else. You-uns had best keep limber, too."

" But what " — Alec began close to his ear, and then there was a step on the ladder.

" All set ! " a voice announced below. " Come down ! "

Alec gave Lafayette's hand a warm squeeze and ran down the ladder. A lumber-wagon was waiting outside the cabin. Jeemes and Kimmell were on the seat, and they had Alec sit between them. Two of the other men climbed in behind, and Jeemes touched the horses with his whip. They plunged off at a good trot, and Alec involuntarily looked up at the stars to see in what direction they were starting.

Kimmell laughed and pulled a handkerchief from his pocket. " Never mind about that," he said, and tied the handkerchief around the boy's eyes. Under all the conditions it was a very natural thing to do, but it made Alec angry at first and then depressed. He was not afraid for himself, but the danger to his uncle began to seem more imminent as he was carried on and on.

And yet several days must pass before anything could be done, and his disappearance would put the doctor on his guard, unless the doctor thought that he had run away. Hutchins's influence might prove stronger, too, than Kimmell's — he started upright, realizing that in the middle of his troubled thought his mind had drifted into unconsciousness and his head had nodded.

"See hyar," said Jeemes, "thar 's straw in the wagon bed. You-uns had better crawl back an' lay down."

Alec crawled back. The road was rough and the thrill of the springless wagon was like that of a steamer in rough sea, but the day and the night had wearied him to the very bone, and in two minutes he was fast asleep. When he woke it was morning, and the wagon was standing beside another cabin door.

CHAPTER IV

IN WHICH PLENTY OF ROPE IS GIVEN TO ALEC

"Boss" JEEMES — whose given name was Boston, no one knew why — was a very tall, thin man with square jaws, hollow cheeks, and a look of having been dipped in a tan vat, — clothes, complexion, and all. The term "butternut," which was applied to Confederate sympathizers within the Union lines, seemed to have been invented on purpose to describe him. He was standing beside the wagon when Alec woke, and his cheerful "Mornin', sonny, mornin,'" was the boy's welcome into captivity.

The handkerchief had worked askew so that Alec could see with one eye. He pulled it off entirely and sat up, feeling sore and battered and dusty, but rousing at once to a full memory of what had happened. The cabin beside which the wagon had halted was the only building in a very small clearing surrounded by thick woods.

Something in the touch of the air and the look of the sky gave a feeling that the land was high rather than low, but there was no outlook of any sort except skyward. A thread of blue smoke from the cabin went straight up to the blue above, and a smell of frying came out of the cabin door. The horses had been unharnessed and tethered to trees, and were eagerly crunching long, hard, white ears of corn. The men themselves lounged around the wagon, looking curiously at Alec while he looked curiously at everything else. Finally he pointed at one of the little patches where a hand-breadth of crop was springing up.

"Do you grow cotton as far north as this?" he asked.

The men laughed aloud. The question of crops seemed irrelevant from a captive, but Hiram Jeemes, who understood the boy's homesickness better than the others, sobered down at once, all but his eyes. "Yes, sonny, that's cotton," he said; "why not? You-uns is in the South now. No use studyin' about how you got here nor where you be. Jus' keep it in yore mind that you-uns is in the South, an' that we-uns is friends."

"'Light, sonny, 'light," added Boss Jeemes cordially. "It does me mighty proud to make yore acquaintance. 'Light an' take a wash. The ole lady'll have breakfast ready mighty soon."

Alec jumped out of the wagon. At a word from Boss, a little girl came from the cabin carrying a big brown gourd of water, which she emptied into a basin near the door. After Alec had soused his face in the basin and cleared the cobwebs from his eyes, he found her still standing and looking at him, as quiet and alert as a rabbit who has heard some one whistle. The day before he had bought a package of candy on the train, and there had been a brass ring in

it with a red glass " jewel." He happened
to have this still in his pocket, and remem-
bering it, he held it out to the child on the
palm of his hand. She only stared at it without drawing any nearer.

Hiram Jeemes came up and looked at it.
" Do you-uns aim for her to take it ? " he
asked.

" Yes, if she wants it," Alec said ; " it 's
shiny yet, but it 's only brass."

" Take it, Virgie, take the pretty from the
young man," Hiram urged.

The child approached slowly, made a timid
but quick and successful reach for the ring,
and ran round the cabin out of sight. Her
father apologized for the shyness which kept
her from showing gratitude, and then his
wife came to the door to ask them all in to
breakfast. She was almost as small and
timid as Virgie, and she did not sit down at
table but waited on the others while they
ate. Although the men who had come with
Alec had taken little or no sleep during the

night, they were all in a genial mood, and Alec felt at home among them.

After breakfast the horses were harnessed again, and three of the men drove away; one, named Johnson, stayed — "to visit Boss," he said. He was a heavy-looking fellow, and presently, as he sat in a chair leaning against the side of the cabin, he fell asleep. Jeemes beckoned silently to Alec, and went out into the edge of the woods where he had felled a tree the day before. Instead of going to work, he put one foot on the low stump, rested one hand and one elbow on his knee, and looked at Alec.

"They tell me you-uns is from Tennessy," he said.

"Yes," Alec answered, sitting down on the log.

"An' you favor the Confeds every time, 'stid of the Yankees."

"Of course; uncle Mortimer is the only abolitionist in our family."

"Then, sonny," said Jeemes, "looks to

me like that-thar Kimmell had better left you be."

"But did n't they tell you?" said Alec. "I happened to overhear their plans for capturing uncle Mortimer, and Kimmell would n't trust me not to go back and tell. It was natural enough."

"Kimmell's a plumb fool," said Boss. "Now I'd have knowed from the looks of you-uns that you would n't go back on yore friends and on the South. Some folks looks like go-betweens an' some don't."

Alec flushed. "Now see here," he said, bringing his brows together in an earnest scowl, "I don't know what I'd have done if they'd left me free. I'm for the South every time, but I can't live with uncle Mortimer and play the spy on him, and I don't believe I could just stay quiet in his house, when I knew there was a plot against him, and wait for him to be captured. I would n't have told him all I knew or how I knew it, but I might have put him on his guard.

Of course, if he was n't going to be hurt, it would n't matter, but some of the men said they did n't expect to take him alive."

" Plenty of men killed in the army on both sides, sonny," Jeemes said.

" But this is different," Alec declared. " You know if you were in my place you 'd think so, too."

Jeemes shifted his position. " I might, sonny, I might," he said. " I don't hold no grudge ag'in ole Doc Ford, nohow. I kin see you-uns would ha' been in a mighty onpleasant fix if you 'd ha' been left to play your own hand. I reckon you 're kind o' glad the boys brung you hyar."

" I don't know about that, either," said Alec. He leaned forward and pried up a loose flake of bark, and then looked straight up into his companion's eyes. " Do you think they 'll do any harm to my uncle if they capture him ? " he asked.

Jeemes put his hand on the boy's shoulder. " As God 's hearin' me, sonny, I don't

know," he said. "I aim to be there and do
my best for the ole doc, for he saved Virgie
to me oncet, but thar 's men among us that
I don't like nor trust. That-thar Kimmell 's
one, and there 's more like him. They 've
got money in Southern bonds, and they
won't stop at nothin'. Johnson in yonder 's
another of 'em, an' they 're gettin' too
strong for the balance of us to hold. We 're
in for anything in the shape of a fair fight,
but there 's some things we can't swaller.
Me an' Hiram are bound to stick by the
order and get these-hyar sharks out 'n the
lead, an' strike a fair blow for the South;
an' if a force of us was to meet up with the
old doc leadin' soldiers ag'in us, that would
be one thing; but ontil he gets the soldiers,
looks to me like he 's jus' the ole doc that 's
nussed us all.

"But that-thar Kimmell would make a
raid on his own mammy, if it would save his
bonds. I 'm tellin' you-uns the truth, sonny,
for I 've got to treat you a way that I don't

like. This-hyar 's a mighty lonesome spot, an' nobody 's likely to come hyar lookin' for you, but if they did, they 'd see you mighty quick if you was anywhere around the clearin', so we 've got to hide you out in the rocks. My orders is to put you there right soon this mornin', before there 's any chance of the old doc's comin' after you; but when Johnson dozed off, I 'lowed I 'd tell you how me an' Hiram an' a lot more looks at things — that 's all.

" We-uns would n't think hard of you if you was to get away, but Johnson 's hyar to see to that, an' it would n't be safe for you afterward, anyhow. Come along; he 'll suspicion something if he wakes up an' we 're gone."

"You 're a mighty good man, Mr. Jeemes," Alec said.

Boss smiled a little and held out a big, sinewy, brown hand. Alec gave it a vigorous shake, and they went back to the cabin.

Johnson was still asleep; Jeemes found

Virgie, and after a whispered consultation the child stole up, touched him on the cheek with a straw, and ran away. He jumped to his feet, looked around him foolishly, and saw Jeemes and Alec standing by, laughing.

" How long is it since the boys left ? " he asked.

" 'Bout half a hour," said Jeemes. " Time we was gettin' this young beanpole out o' sight." He went into the cabin and came out with a big coil of rope, a bottle of water, and a corn-cake. The provisions went into Alec's pockets, and Jeemes thrust his arm through the coil of rope. " Many a man from the 109th that was tired of fightin' ag'in the South has found this-hyar rope mighty handy before now," he declared. " You-uns ain't the first feller that has been hid out in the Pine Hills."

" No use naming any names," said Johnson.

Boss was leading the way across the clearing. He looked back at Alec. "You-uns is jus' as wise when I say 'Sycamore Flats,' ain't you, sonny?" he said.

"Just exactly," agreed Alec. "I was brought like a cat in a bag, and I don't know whether I'm north, south, east, or west of North Pass. I only guess from the time that we came fifteen or twenty miles and are still in Illinois."

The men made no answer, but entered the woods and went picking their way through the undergrowth, taking care to leave as little trail as possible. Here and there gnarled old pines stood among the deciduous trees, but Alec paid little attention to them, not knowing that among all the things which had impressed him as Southern, these were the most Southern of all, being of a Southern species and marking a little belt where the flora is more like that of Mississippi than of Illinois or even of Tennessee.

They grew more abundant as the party

moved forward, and finally the rest of the
forest gave way, and left the old pine-trees
standing alone on the edge of a cliff which
made an abrupt and unexpected end to the
hill country and the forest. The rocks were
of gray limestone, and where the line of
bluff turned a little so that its sheer wall
came in sight, Alec saw that it was hoary
with lichens and water-worn into impressive
forms.

Nothing could be more different from the
hills on Doctor Ford's place, and he began
to wonder if he was a good deal more than
twenty miles from North Pass. At the foot
of the cliff was a marshy lake, so green with
water-plants that the water scarcely showed.
The outlet of the lake made a rift through
the masses of lowland forest which closed it
around its farther shore, and through this
rift there was a glimpse of a distant river.

Alec pointed to it. " Is that the Mississippi or the Ohio ? " he asked.

" Just as you please," answered Jeemes.

" You 're going to have all day to study on which it favors most. Come hyar."

Alec went to the place where Jeemes was standing, on the extreme edge of the bluff. Jeemes pointed to a small scrag of pine which grew far down the face of the rock. " Can you-uns see a little holler scooped into the rock behind that piney ? " he asked. " It 's big enough for a man to lie in right comf'table, an' anybody we-uns wants safe out o' sight we lowers down thar. We 'll let you up every night to stretch yourse'f a spell, an' if things look peaceable mebbe you can sleep in the cabin. It ain't such hard lines. Anyhow, me an' Johnson cain't be kep' home day an' night to watch you-uns, so that 's whar you 've got to go."

Johnson took the rope and slipped it under Alec's arms. " It ain't much to ask of you for a good cause," he said. " When you 're safely landed, untie the rope so we can pull it up."

" All right," said Alec, and the two men

let him carefully down until he found a foothold beside the little pine-tree, and crept into the nook which some chance of nature had hollowed out of the rock. Then he untied the rope, the men withdrew it, bade him good-by jocosely, and went away.

When they had been gone a little while, Alec leaned out upon the pine, found that it would bear his weight, and then crept out and sat upon it to take a good survey of the situation.

For a long way there were no footholds on the rock, and he was surprised at the great height of the bluff. About as far below him as he was from the top of the rocks there was a ledge on which one might stand, and below that the face of the rock was diversified by fissures, in some of which fallen fragments had lodged or trees had taken root, so that from above it looked like an easy descent from the ledge to the level of the lake. But there seemed to be no possibility of getting to the ledge, and

"THAT'S WHAR YOU 'VE GOT TO GO"

so Alec crept back into the little place where he had been pigeon-holed for future reference, and gazed out over the broad, densely wooded bottom-lands.

A few thin fleeces of smoke moved along the sky, marking the course of the river, and while he watched them he realized that as the river lay to the west, it must be the Mississippi, and he must still be in Illinois. It was a little comfort to be sure of what State he was in, and to know that North Pass was somewhere to the east of him, and probably not more than twenty miles away.

He remembered that his uncle had said the flag could be seen for twenty miles, and it occurred to him that it was probably in sight from these Pine Hills, if he could only climb up into some tree high enough to let him see out over the forest. The idea excited him, and although there seemed to be no prospect of climbing anywhere except on his stunted " piney," it gave him something to think of while he let the hours pass.

About mid-afternoon he heard a slight stir above him. He crept out along the pine trunk and looked up. There stood Virgie Jeemes, holding by a bush at the very edge of the cliff, and leaning over to look at him ; even the impassable distance between them did not give her full confidence, and he had scarcely seen her before she ran away. But after a little while her small white face parted the branches of the bush and peered down again, and soon she thrust out one hand with the ring hanging like a hoop from her forefinger.

" Thanky ! " she ventured.

" You 're mighty welcome," he answered. " It 's most big enough for two of your fingers."

" Pappy says they 'll grow to it," she said ; and then leaning a little farther out of the bush she whispered, " Pappy 's gone."

" Where ? "

She shook her head. " Him an' Mr. Johnson went right soon after they brung

you-uns hyar.   They 'lowed they 'd be back
'fore dark, but I dunno where they went.
They don't never tell."   She twirled the
ring on her finger wistfully, and there was
a gap in the interview.

"How did you find your way out here?"
Alec finally asked.

"Follered after you-uns an' pappy this
morning," she explained, and then she looked
at the glittering ring again.   "It's mighty
pretty."

Alec smiled up at her.   She had evidently
come out on purpose to make friends with
him, out of gratitude, but she was almost too
shy.   "Want to do something for me?"
he asked, with no purpose beyond an idle
impulse.

She nodded her head energetically.

"Then wait a minute."   He crawled
back into his retreat and brought out his
water-bottle.   "See, it's empty," he said,
"but I think your pappy left his rope
up there under a bush, and if you 'll find it

and let it down to me, I 'll tie the bottle on
and you can pull it up and fill it fresh for
me ; do you think you can ? "

She nodded her head again, and began to
search for the rope.   In a moment she found
it under a bush and began letting it down ;
as the end dangled toward Alec, his boyish
scheme for doing something to set the child
at ease and break the monotony developed a
possibility which he had not dreamed of at
the first.

" Be careful ! " he called.   " I 'm afraid
you 'll fall over, if you stand up like that.
Lie flat on the rock."

She lay down, and then he made her draw
back until her big, wondering eyes no longer
peered over the edge, and he could see nothing of her but her brown hands paying
out the rope.

" That 's right ; I 'll tell you when it 's
down far enough," he assured her, but he
did not say a word until she had let it down
as far as she could and the end was in her

hands. Then he asked her not to move until he could tie the bottle on. For a moment he fumbled with the rope, then jerked it suddenly out of her grasp.

As it slipped rattling down the face of the cliff, Virgie crawled to the edge and stared after it in consternation. Alec was looking up at her ruefully. " I 'd like to know how I 'm going to get my water now," he said. " What made you let go like that ? "

She gazed back without a word, and presently two big tears welled up into her eyes ; she lifted her head, glanced round her through their blur, and then jumped up and ran away from the mischief she had done.

Alec was sure she did not understand the real importance of what had happened, but her pathetic little face reproached him for having taken advantage of her. " Virgie ! " he called, " Virgie ! " but she did not come back to be comforted ; so after a little while he gave up calling, tied the rope to the

" piney," and went down hand over hand to the ledge. He was free to go wherever he could.

From the ledge the way to the foot of the cliff looked more difficult than he had thought, but after a little reconnoitring he found a place at one end of the ledge where he could make his way directly back to the top of the rocks. It was a sharp scramble, and he reached the top panting and almost bewildered by the suddenness with which his escape had come about.

Virgie was nowhere to be seen, and he paused a moment to get breath. It was late afternoon, and the sun was sinking fast, its light falling across the lowland forests in visible shafts of gold. There was not a sign of habitation anywhere, only a broad, out-spreading loneliness. He turned with a friendless feeling, and went back into the woods, scanning every tree.

After a while he found one which seemed to overtop the rest, but was not too large for him to climb ; he climbed it, and when he reached the very topmost branch, straightened himself and looked out toward the east. At first glance the highland forests appeared almost as unbroken as those of the lowlands, but in the distance he could make out many little gaps which he knew must mean homesteads, and from one hilltop on the horizon line the sunlight glinted back in small, red sparks from the windows of a house, although the house itself could not be seen.

He remembered how the trees stood guard around Doctor Ford's stone cottage, hiding it, and he scanned the sky-line of the trees through which these windows gleamed. In one spot the line rose high into the bluish haze, and from its highest point a fleck of brightness twinkled a moment, was lost, and then twinkled into sight again, and he knew it was the flag !

He choked a little as he made sure of his bearings, noting the trend of valleys and hill ranges, and when he had taken the long slide down the trunk from the branches to the ground, and stood brushing off the bark dust, he muttered : —

"I never expected to be so glad to see that flag."

CHAPTER V

WHEN Doctor Ford and T. D. came home
from their fruitless search for meetings of
the Golden Circle, on the night after Alec's
arrival, the doctor went softly to the door
of the room he had assigned to Alec, and
tapped. There was no answer. He took a
lamp, and entered the room. It was empty,
and showed no sign of Alec's having as
much as entered it.

The doctor turned sharply and found that
T. D. had come in, too, and was standing
behind him, looking confounded.

" He 's run away," the doctor said. " Too
much of a rebel to stay with us."

T. D. rubbed his brow. " Mebbe not,"
he said ; " mebbe he 's jus' stickin' clost to
Lafayette."

" Lafayette ? " said the doctor. " What do you mean ? "

T. D. blinked a little and tried to swallow the distaste of a confession. " I mean I'm a plumb coward," he blurted desperately, " an' so 's Lafayette. He deserted, an' I hid him out in the cave."

" And Alec ? " asked the doctor, compressing his lips.

" I reckon he 's down there in the cave takin' care of him now," T. D. answered. " Lafayette was about to die " —

The doctor turned away from him, and started out of the house.

T. D. followed. " If I tell you how it was," he began, " you-uns won't think quite so hard of me, doc " —

" I don't care how it was," the doctor asserted over his shoulder, in a tone which left nothing more to be said.

The two men hastened across the lawn and through the peach orchard in silence, taking the shortest way to the cave.

" We put him in the top barrel on account of the other one being so damp," T. D. explained, as they went through the gap.

" Very thoughtful," the doctor answered dryly. " Pity you did n't honor me as a physician, if not as an old acquaintance."

" You see, doc, it was this-a-way," T. D. hastened to begin again ; " jus' when I found Lafayette " —

" But I don't care how it was," the doctor repeated. He took a small dark lantern out of his coat, and opening it, lighted their way around the pool and up to the second chamber of the cave. When he threw the light into it, it was as tenantless as the bedroom in the house, but he was too angry to be exactly surprised or alarmed. He merely turned to T. D. " Well ? " he asked.

T. D. looked round and round the cave, unable to believe that it was vacant. Finally he saw the half-burned match which Alec had thrown down. He picked it up and held it toward the doctor.

" Well ? " the doctor insisted.

" I 'm beat," said T. D.

" Then this was n't part of your programme ? "

" Nope," T. D. answered. He rubbed his forehead again as if trying to make sure of what he remembered. " He dropped in the ravine, an' me an' Alec toted him to the gap," he said slowly. " I sprinkled his face, an' he come to enough to help himself a little climbin' up hyar, an' we laid him on the warm stones an' left him. When we got to the house, I did up a blanket an' some grub for Alec to bring back to him after we-uns had left, an' that 's all I know."

" In that case," the doctor declared, " it must be as I said at first. Alec has run away."

" An' what about Lafayette ? " asked T. D. ; " he had n't strength enough to go any farther."

" And yet you see he 's gone," answered the doctor, " strength or no strength. I suppose he thought my cave was n't a very healthy place to be hiding in."

" But I don't know where they 'd go to," T. D. objected.

" That 's a question which does n't interest me," the doctor answered. " It 's their own affair, as long as they 've chosen to go. I shall not look for them."

" But, doc," — T. D. began.

The doctor made an impatient movement. " I don't want to hear you ! " he said. " You have deceived me without cause, and I know you 'll not do it again, so there 's nothing more to be discussed about that. As for Lafayette, if you had told me he was here and sick, I should have taken care of him, and then had him restored to the army with as little dishonor as possible. You did n't trust me and he did n't trust you, so that account is closed, and he can shift for himself ; this is not a hard neighborhood for a deserter to find shelter in. About Alec " —

He paused abruptly, for his voice was on

the point of quivering. It had been pleasant
to think that his brother's son was to live
with him, and there had been something
about the boy which had assured him that
they would understand each other and be
friends, in spite of all their differences.

"Looks like we had n't ought to let him
go," T. D. ventured.

"I would n't talk about letting him go,"
the doctor blazed out. "If he 'd seen that
we stood by each other and were to be de-
pended on, he might have stayed, but what
was there to make him stay when we were
not only working against his cause, but
against each other? No, I 'll not take a
step to bring him back. He did n't like the
prospect ahead of him, and he left. Now
we 'll go on as before. There 's no more to
be said."

T. D.'s face was as furrowed and twisted as
it had been when he whistled, but now there
was perplexity and remorse in every line.
He had meant so little harm that it seemed

as if there must be some way to set everything right, but as he went all over the situation, he could find no means for allaying the doctor's anger or comforting him, and there was nothing he could do but follow the doctor's tall figure back toward the house, walking close enough to reach out and touch him, but carrying the weight of impassable barriers in his consciousness.

It was a bitter state of things, after they had lived twenty years together, not as master and servant, but as friends. Suddenly he stopped short. " I can't stan' it doc," he declared. " Give me the lantern. I 'm going back to try to trace them two an' bring 'em home. They hain't gone fur — not if they 've kep' together, fer Lafayette was too weak."

The doctor handed him the lantern. T. D. hesitated a moment. " I don't like to go off an' leave you-uns," he went on, " but things look to be mighty quiet, an' I won't be gone long. If I don't find 'em soon, I 'll come back."

" Don't hurry on my account," the doctor
said. " It's just as well to have the last one
of you gone, and be done with it. I wish
you a pleasant journey."

" But, doc!" T. D. expostulated.

The doctor paid no attention, and strode
off, leaving T. D. to turn the other way and
go back with a sore heart to the cave.

The doctor, himself, was very miserable.
He was disappointed and hurt all the way
through, and more than that, he knew he
had been brutal to T. D., who had never
failed him before, and never would again.
He knew he would have to forgive T. D.
some time, but the knowledge only made
him feel angrier for the present, and he put
his head forward and rushed up the hill as
if he were charging an enemy.

As he came out into the lawn, he caught
sight of a figure moving among the trees.
For a moment his mood lightened, for he
thought it was Alec, home again after all.

" Hello!" he called.

" Hello ! " a voice answered — not Alec's.

" Who are you and what do you want ? " the doctor asked in a different tone.

" I 'm Hutchins," the man answered, coming toward him through the obscurity of the starlight.

" Oh ! " said the doctor.   He had been prepared to meet some new emergency of border warfare, and he was recalled instead to one of those heart-breaking cases which physicians know, and at thought of which they cease to be anything but physicians.

He and Hutchins were enemies in politics, yet night after night they had fought side by side for a life which was more to Hutchins than his own, but which no doctor's skill could hold for very long.   A thin, white face rose before the doctor, the eyes brilliant with pain, and begging him for some relief.

" Is it one of her worst turns ? " he asked. " Have you been waiting long ? "

Hutchins answered in an oddly husky voice.   " My wife is not suffering to-night," he answered. "I came to you on another matter."

"Yes?"

"It's your nephew," Hutchins went on. "Don't worry about him. He's safe. I come to warn you not to hunt for him. You might get yourself in trouble."

"Humph! Trouble is something I'm noted for avoiding," the doctor scoffed. "How did he smell out you copperheads so quick? I told him you existed, but I did n't give him your addresses. I suppose it was n't necessary. What they call an affinity guided him to his friends."

"Perhaps so," answered Hutchins, twisting his hands, "but the boy's not staying away of his own free will. He'll not be hurt, but he was taken possession of because he happened to overhear a plot against your liberty if not your life. It was n't considered safe to let him come back to you after that. He was too likely to warn you."

The doctor gave a little laugh. "What

are you doing ? " he asked. " Look here,
Hutchins, you ought n't to do things like
this. You 've relieved me about the boy ;
I thought he had run away, and I did n't like
it. But you take a risk in coming straight
to me from one of your meetings. Somebody may keep watch of you. Don't do it
again."

Hutchins laid a hand on the doctor's
shoulder for an instant, and the doctor noticed that the hand was trembling. " Then
promise me to be on your guard," he begged,
"and if it comes to close quarters, don't resist.
If your house is raided, it will be by a party
strong enough to take you dead or alive, so
you might as well yield peaceably. There 's
not one of them that wishes you harm on
personal grounds, but killing a man does n't
seem quite the same in war time as in time
of peace. They 're desperate and bound to
win."

" So am I," the doctor declared. " It 's
no use talking to me of not resisting. People

who give up never know what they might have won, and if a man begins the business of giving up, he might as well be dead, and done with it."

Hutchins was silent several moments. " I can't stand it, doc," he began at last, speaking slowly to keep his voice steady. " I don't know where the right of things is any more, but I know the things I can do and the things I can't, and I reckon the best we can do sometimes is to stick by our instincts and not try to reason too far. God knows I believe in the cause of the South, and I thought I could help it by joining the Knights, but there are men stronger than I am in the council that advocate things I can't help to carry through. For the last two or three months I 've only stood by the order to try to hold it in check, and now I 'm done. If you 're going to make a fight of it, you 'll find me fighting on your side."

The doctor took a step closer to him. " Hutchins," he said, " don't give up the cause you believe in on my account. I would n't for any man."

"I don't give up the cause," Hutchins answered, "I only give up trying to serve it where there's no honorable way. And then, doc, there are things between us" — His voice choked up, and he held out his hand to save the need of words. The doctor clasped it, accepting his allegiance with it, and each felt the strength and earnestness of the other in his grip.

"When will the raid be?" the doctor asked presently.

"I don't know," said Hutchins. "There's to be a final discussion of it to-morrow night. It will be soon, but not for two or three days, I think, on account of communicating with parties across the river. You'll have time to get help up from Cairo."

"Soldiers are all very well for capturing deserters, but I don't want any to protect me," the doctor asserted, rousing into his stubborn tone again. "If I had soldiers

once, I should have to have them all the
time, and to live under protection would be
one way of giving up. I'd rather take my
chances as usual."

Hutchins shook his head in discourage-
ment. Even with his help, there would be
only three men against twenty. "Where is
T. D. ?" he asked, missing him for the first
time.

"He started off trying to track Alec and
Lafayette. A fool's errand, but he was
bound to go. Is Lafayette all right?"

"He's perfectly safe," answered Hutchins.
"He's a very sick man, but he's in good
care, and you would n't be permitted to see
him if you knew where he is, for he over-
heard the same things as Alec. I wish we
could get T. D. back from looking for them,
but T. D. 's not likely to get hurt. He's
sharper than you are, doc, by half."

The doctor hitched his shoulders. "T. D.
can look out for himself," he declared.
"And as for you, you'd better go back

home. I don't need you to-night, and I don't much approve of your mixing yourself in this affair. Your wife's too sick."

"I'm going back now," Hutchins said, "but I'll be here again. Whenever I can leave her. Good-night."

They shook hands once more. Hutchins started away, and was soon lost in the dusk. The doctor went into the house, and to bed, but it was daybreak before he slept.

Some time in the afternoon he was roused by a voice calling, "Hello!" from outside. The doctor sprang to his feet, dressed hurriedly, and went to the door.

A man from a remote settlement was waiting for him with a summons. He looked through his medicine-bag to see if he had everything he needed, pinned a notice on the door to tell other comers that he would not be back until next day, went to the barn for his horse, and started off with the man who had come for him.

About halfway down the hill he reined

in abruptly. " Here comes Hi Jeemes," he said to his companion ; " I 'll wait to speak to him."

" Howdy, doc," Jeemes called, in something graver than his usual easy voice.

" How are you," the doctor returned. " Anybody sick at your house ? "

" No, not now," Jeemes answered, " but I 'm glad I did n't miss you." He looked the doctor over with his imperturbably bright, blue eyes. " The fact is, T. D.'s Lafayette took refuge at my house last night. He was mighty sick, an' I had ought to ha' let you-uns know first thing, but I 'lowed that being as he had left the army " —

" What 's the short of it ? " asked the doctor. " I 'm on my way to a serious case. Is he still there ? "

" Doc," said Hiram gently, " he 's thar, but he 's dead."

" What ! " cried the doctor. He turned and looked at the man beside him, as if asking a release.

The man leaned toward him imploringly.

"My child 'll die if we don't get thar, doc," he urged. "You-uns cain't do no more 'n other folks fer a dead man."

"That's true enough," the doctor acknowledged. "Hiram, can't you attend to everything for me, and send round the neighborhood after T. D.? He's out somewhere searching for Lafayette, and when you find him tell him you saw me, and tell him "— He paused, thinking of the night before, and that his going now might seem like an added harshness. He flushed a little and his eyes sparkled with the courage for sending a message of sympathy through Hiram Jeemes. "Tell him how it was, Hi," he said brusquely, "and tell him my heart's with him like it's been for twenty years. Say it in just those words — you understand?"

Hiram nodded. "I won't ferget 'em," he declared, "an' I'll tend to everything What time 'll you-uns git home?"

" Not before to-morrow morning anyhow, and maybe not so soon. Don't wait for me if I don't come. T. D. 'll understand."

" All right," Jeemes agreed.

" Then good-by," said the doctor, and he and his companion galloped away. It was not the first time in his busy practice that he had slighted death for the sake of sickness. The thought of Lafayette's lonely death and of T. D. haunted him. Then the man who had come for him rode alongside and began to tell him more details about the sick child, and the doctor forced himself to put away every consideration of what he had left behind. Before sunset he was as far to the east of North Pass as Alec was to the west, and when Alec was looking from his tree-top on the Pine Hills, the flag was beckoning from a deserted place.

During all of the following night the doctor kept vigil, and when he was obliged to take rest the next morning, the crisis had not been reached. It was not until toward evening that he found the child out of danger and was able to start for home.

There had been a heavy rain during the day, and the roads were a thin batter of mud, which splashed over him at every step. The little runs which crossed his way were high, and the night was black. The ride was long, and seemed longer, for his mind ran ahead of him all the way. He had no reason now to be in haste, for the last words must have been spoken hours before over poor Lafayette, but somehow he could not keep from urging his horse forward with the same sense of strain as when he was riding to a case of life or death.

At last he closed the gate of his own place behind him, and felt with sympathy the eagerness with which his horse scrambled up the slippery road; they were both thankful to be getting home, and as they neared the top of the hill, the doctor kept looking ahead, hoping to see a light in the house.

" Ah ! " he muttered in relief, catching a

flash of brightness through the trees. Then he saw that the light was outside of the house, and he began to hear excited voices. There were several men standing around the flag-tree, and suddenly there was a crack of breaking wood and all the men cried out together. Something heavy, like a straight limb, was thrown out from the top of the tree, and as it fell it unfurled and caught the lantern light, below.

The doctor put spurs to his horse. The Knights of the Golden Circle had come for him, and not finding him, they had brought down the flag.

CHAPTER VI

Boss JEEMES and Johnson returned to Jeemes's rather early, the evening after they had put Alec into the nook on the side of the cliff. Mrs. Jeemes met them with a frightened face, and told them the story which Virgie had finally told her, and they hurried out to the bluff and found Alec gone. Johnson was suspicious and angry; there were hot words between him and Jeemes, but nothing could be done except to ride back in haste to the council of the Golden Circle, which met that night, and advise an immediate raid before Alec could reach Doctor Ford's, and the doctor could send for assistance.

But Hiram Jeemes was at the council with the news of Lafayette's death and the doc-

tor's absence. The raid was postponed until
the night following, when the doctor would
probably have returned, and it was agreed
that if he was not in the house when they
surrounded it, they would conceal themselves
and wait for him. In the mean time, Lafayette's burial had to be attended to in the
afternoon, for T. D. had not come back,
and no one knew what had become of him
or where to look, and the doctor's return
was likely to be too late.

They all felt the ironical sadness of the situation, and for the brief interlude of the
funeral they ceased to be enemies of the
dead man and his friends, and were simply
neighbors gathered together in kindliness
under a gray sky in the rain. After night-
fall it was with an odd change of mood
that they assembled on the hilltop, and
having nothing else to do before going into
ambush, threw down the flag.

Alec had passed the night before in a dry
ravine under a drift of leaves, sleeping

uneasily and waiting for light to travel by;
but when light came the rain began, and it
kept him floundering nearly all day through
the woods, hungry, cold, discouraged, and
lost again and again because he could get
no outlook over the country. Finally he
came to a road, and decided to follow it, in
spite of the risk of its going the wrong way,
and of his meeting some one he knew upon
it. He was not mistaken in thinking that
it led toward North Pass, and the two or
three people whom he might have met he
managed to avoid by slipping back among
the trees.

Toward night he came upon a little clearing and a house close by the road, and a
woman who had come out to the fence to
call her cows up from the woods. She saw
him, so he made the best of it by inquiring
his way and asking for something to eat.
She brought him food willingly, saying a
word or two which showed that she thought
he might be a deserter from the army. He

was glad enough to be accounted for in that way, but he went on without stopping to rest and dry himself as she advised, fearing to find one of his Golden Circle friends inside.

The rain stopped, and although night came, he could still follow the road. At last he saw the handful of scattered lights which marked North Pass. Skirting slowly around the village, he found the road again on the other side, and hastened on over the ground he had traversed on his way up from the train.

When he was in the woods just below the entrance to his uncle's place, he heard a man running behind him, and he stepped to one side. The man was carrying a lantern, so that Alec saw him plainly as he came near. It was Hutchins, hatless and coatless, his face wearing that wild, unbalanced look which shows that a single grief or fear has driven all other thoughts out of the mind.

Alec sprang into the road and caught him

by the arm. " Has anything happened to my uncle ? " he asked.

Hutchins looked at him without recognition for a moment, and then shook him off. " Your uncle 's been gone nearly two days, and my wife 's been worse," he answered, starting on.

Alec kept alongside, catching hold of Hutchins again to claim his attention. " Uncle Mortimer has n't been captured, has he ? " he asked.

Hutchins did not shake him off this time. Something in the boy's white face caught his notice and claimed his sympathy. " No, no, doc has n't been captured," he answered kindly ; " he 'll be glad to see you home. They won't raid him for two or three days yet, thank God ! but he 's been off to attend a sick child. If he 's not back now, my wife will die — she may die before I get home."

They had reached the gate of the doctor's place. " Don't come any farther ! " Alec begged. "If my uncle's here, I'll send him. I'll send him whenever he comes. You won't need to come away again."

"You understand that you're to give the message on the instant?" Hutchins asked. "That she's at the point of death?"

"Oh, yes, yes," Alec promised. "Trust me — no matter what he's doing, he will come."

Hutchins turned without a word and rushed down the hill. Alec had never seen any one so nearly crazed with suffering before, and Hutchins's face and voice seemed to goad him forward as he ran up the hill. But when he came to the edge of the lawn on the hilltop, they were suddenly driven from his mind. The space under the flag-tree was full of lights and figures; he heard a crash and shouts, and saw a man ride out of a shadow in front of him and spur his horse straight for the centre of the group.

"Pick up that flag!" he heard his uncle shout.

It was never Alec's way to consider if it were prudent to throw himself into the thick of things. He followed his uncle at full speed, and the group of men opened a little to let them in, then closed around them. The doctor jumped from his horse and picked up the flag himself. " This is going back to its place ! " he announced. " Who's up in the tree? Who sawed off the flag ? "

" I don't reckon that makes much difference to you-uns, doc," Hiram Jeems apologized, stepping toward him. " We-uns have brought you an invite to a trip with us tonight. You're needed mighty bad on the Kaintucky shore."

" Thank you," answered the doctor, " but I shall sleep at home. It's the first time I ever refused one of you, boys, you'll admit that; but I think this case can wait — till the judgment-day."

Hiram came a little nearer, trying to make his face express the wisdom of yielding. " Think twicet 'bout'n it, doc," he said anxiously. " Thar 's twenty on us hyar, all axin' you to go."

" There may be forty of you, for all I care," Doctor Ford declared, " but I 'll not go, either on a pretense or any other way. You have a nice style of putting things, Hiram, but I can tell you that if you want to take me to-night, you 'll take me dead ! "

The man who was in the tree began to come down hastily, and the doctor sprang back against the trunk, pulling Alec with him, to prevent an attack from behind. " Is that you, Kimmell ? " he asked. " I supposed you were at the head of this affair."

Kimmell reached ground on the other side of the tree, threw away his saw, and drew his revolver. The doctor stood unarmed, knowing that one against so many could accomplish nothing by menace, and Alec had no weapon. One of the men led the horse out of the way, tethering it at some distance, and Kimmell walked round the tree.

" There 's no use wasting words," he said.

" You've got to go with us peaceably or by force.   You may take your choice."

" I don't choose to do either," the doctor answered, in his stubborn voice.   " I intend to stay right here, and not one of you dares to level your revolver at me in cold blood and shoot.   You might just as well give up and go home."

There was a pause, and Alec could hear his heart beating so loudly that he felt as if every one else must hear it and think he was afraid; but there was nothing he could do or say to help his uncle, and the men scarcely seemed to notice that he was there.   They were looking questioningly from one to another, and if any one had appealed to them at that moment, recalling all that the doctor had undergone for them, and all the tenderness which showed so seldom in his speech, there was scarcely one among them who could have kept from going up and clutching his hand and telling him that he was too brave a man to harm.

But the doctor was too angry to make appeals. He stood among them erect and defiant, with Alec, who should have been safe in the Pine Hills, close beside him, offering a fresh testimony to his influence ; and yet his sudden appearance among them, and his assertion of himself, had put them all on the footing of man to man, and from that standpoint it was hard to move. They wished he had not spoken to them about shooting in cold blood, or that so many of them did not owe him their lives.

Kimmell was one of the few in whom there was no wavering. His laugh broke the silence confidently. " Well, boys, you 're easily scared," he said. " Nobody wants to shoot him ! Just close in and capture him and this young friend of ours who ' belongs to the South.' "

Still the men hesitated, and when the doctor's horse gave a shrill, protesting whinny, every one of them started and looked over his shoulder ; and their long, black shadows, radiating from the centre of lantern-light, carried the stir back into the general darkness. Kimmell grew alarmed. He had come undisguised and fearless, for there would be nobody to call him to account after the doctor was gone, and his plans had not included the possibility that twenty men might yield to one.

"What!" he cried angrily. "Are you afraid of him — afraid to take him because he does n't choose to go?"

He waited another instant and then leaned forward, concealing his sudden fear under the imperious earnestness which was so hard to doubt, and which had led them so often before.

"You are forgetting the South," he began. "They are giving their blood like water there, and their own brothers are not too great a sacrifice, if they meet them on the other side. There are harder things asked of us than personal gratitude, and you know what we might do here, and who stands in our way. You know the difference there will be in this end of the State if he is out of it. We 'll have freedom to follow our own convictions then. We 'll be rid of spies and intimidation " —

" Be careful! " the doctor interrupted, just as he would have warned a man who was about to lose his footing. " I 'm not going with you, and you might say things which would make interesting testimony before some court."

It was a fault of the doctor's courage that it never foresaw the consequence of pushing an enemy to the wall. Kimmell's face turned livid. " Who says you are not going with us? " he demanded. " Do you think you 'll have a chance to testify in any court ? "

He raised his revolver and aimed it steadily, trusting his followers to see that they had gone too far for turning back, but trusting no one to be true to him if the doctor escaped. " Who says you are not coming

"I GIVE YOU ANOTHER MINUTE TO YIELD"·

with us?" he repeated. "I give you another minute to yield."

Boss and Hiram Jeemes sprang forward, forgetting all allegiance to the Knights, but other men grappled with them, and the whole circle broke into a hand-to-hand struggle between the two factions which made it up, while Kimmell, keeping clear of the *mêlée*, still pointed his revolver at the doctor and began to count off the seconds. The Jeemes party was so outnumbered that not one of its members could free himself, and the sweat burst out over them as they fought, for they could catch glimpses of the doctor's stern, white face, and they knew he would not yield.

When death had threatened them instead of him, it had been their watchword that he never would give up. "Boys," Hiram screamed, wrenching furiously against the men who overpowered him, "boys, we can't let him shoot the old doc!"

No one had laid a hand on Alec, he had

stood so still, but at Jeemes's cry he jumped between Kimmell and the doctor. " Promise not to testify against them, uncle Mortimer!" he begged. "Oh, promise not to testify, and they 'll let you go !"

" I 'll promise nothing," the doctor began, " and if Kimmell shoots me " —

Some of the men had seized Alec, and were pulling him out of range, while Kimmell went on counting. The doctor's voice trembled ; for a moment death seemed too hard to bear. He looked after Alec, wondering what the end would be for him, and then he straightened back against the tree.

" Take the boy out of sight!" Johnson said to the men who were holding Alec.

Nothing had seemed real to Alec before, but at Johnson's words he knew that his uncle would be killed, and he felt himself turn sick and faint. All the love that might have grown between them in years awoke in him, and he stretched out his arms with unspeakable longing as he was dragged away.

"Good-by, uncle Mortimer!" he called. "Good-by!"

He heard the crash of a pistol, and then the lights around him all went out, and he sank into darkness, clutching at a curious thought: "When I die, I want to die like that! I don't want to be afraid — oh, I don't want to be afraid!"

Some one grasped him by the shoulder. "Brace up! ole doc 's not killed!" he heard. "Hutchins knocked the revolver out of Kimmell's hand."

It was the first time that Alec had remembered the message he had had no chance to give. He struggled to his feet, realizing that Hutchins must have turned again, after leaving him, and followed up the hill to make sure that there was no delay. His uncle was standing just as before, but Hutchins was between him and Kimmell, and the men had relaxed their hold of one another to stare at his agonized face.

"Oh, for the love of God," he cried

hoarsely, " you can't refuse to let him go to my wife ! She's dying, and I promised her to bring him home."

Boss Jeemes went up to Hutchins and laid a hand on his shoulder. " Don't give up," he said. " Ole doc has saved her before, an' he can save her agin. The boys will let him go."

The doctor leaned the flag against the tree. " That's right, Boss, I hope I can save her," he said; " but I ask no man's permission to go where I am needed. Take care of Alec. I must get my horse."

He picked up a lantern and walked away, for he had been called, and it was his profession to answer. There was but one way in which he could be stopped.

" Johnson ! " shouted Kimmell.

Johnson's revolver flashed into the lantern-light, but Hutchins sprang in front of him and stood before them all, wringing his hands in a piteous effort to find words. Suddenly his drawn face quivered and the tears rolled down his cheeks. "Oh, I promised her!" was all he could say. "I promised her to bring him home!"

Johnson's arm fell, and in the intense pause which followed they could hear the doctor speaking to his horse. Hutchins lifted his head and rushed away into the darkness as swiftly as he had come, and Johnson turned to Kimmell.

"The game's up," he said gruffly. "We might as well make up our minds to it. Ford is stronger than we are, and the Golden Circle's dead around North Pass."

Kimmell looked from man to man. "Boys, is that so?" he asked.

One by one they nodded their heads. "Yes," they said, "it's so. The Golden Circle's dead around North Pass."

Their old leader pulled his hat over his eyes. "All right," he muttered, "you won't see me after this." But the men paid no attention as he turned away. They were watching the doctor's lantern swinging like a signal as his horse splashed off at a gallop down the hill.

" I hope he gets thar in time," said Hiram Jeemes.

For half an hour they stood talking to Alec and to one another of all that had happened, and of all that might happen before the war was ended ; of where T. D. could have gone, about Lafayette's death, and Alec's escape from the cliff.   They praised Alec for his pluck in getting home and in daring to show himself among them, but to Alec there seemed nothing worthy of praise but his uncle's courage.

At last they dispersed by twos and threes, and Alec was left alone.   He picked up the flag wearily, folded it around its staff, and went into the house.   He was thinking of what the men had said about giving up the cause they wished to serve.

" It 's true," he told himself, as he looked around the familiar room which he had seen so little.   " We 're on the wrong side of the line. We can hope, but there's not much we can do." He stood a moment, and mingled with his relief for his uncle the love of his old home rose in him until his eyes brimmed with it. He dropped on his knees beside the bed and buried his face on his arms.

"O God," he sobbed, "we can't do anything here! You must take care of the South!"

In the early morning voices wakened him. "Yes, I 'lowed they might ha' gone to uncle Wash Sanford's out in Johnsing," T. D. was saying. "I could n't study out no other place fer 'em to head. I 'lowed I'd ketch up with 'em on the path through Owl Holler, fer I knowed pore Lafayette would take that way, an' when I did n't find 'em, I jus' kep' on. It's a right smart ways out to uncle Wash's. I stopped thar to get my breath a leetle, an' then I slipped an' sprained my ankle hurryin' back, an' that's why I'm so behind."

"T. D.," the doctor began, "I was afraid I'd driven you away for good, and then when I had to go off after Lafayette died" —

"Doc," T. D. broke in, "Lafayette did n't desert. When Hi Jeemes found me this mornin', that was the first word he spoke. Lafayette tole him before he died. Don't matter much about anything else, now I know he did n't desert an' you ain't mad."

"No," the doctor said, "it does n't even matter that the flag is down, and I don't believe I'll put it up again. I don't want to fly it in their faces after the way they let me off last night to save Hutchins's wife."

"Mebbe 't would be kindest not to," T. D. admitted ruefully.

Alec had been tumbling into his clothes as fast as he could. He burst through the door. "They would n't like it!" he declared. "It would n't seem like your place, and I'm going to put it up!"

His uncle came toward him. "I've got an apology to make to you," he said. "Before Hutchins came and told me what had happened, I thought you'd run away. I know you better now."

Alex flushed with pleasure and wrung his uncle's hand.

"And I know you," he said. "It was splendid the way you walked off last night, with Kimmell ordering them to shoot you in the back!"

"An' I wa'n't there!" T. D. groaned. "I jus' stopped" —

The doctor and Alec burst out laughing. "Of course you stopped," the doctor said.

Mary Tracy Earle (1864–1955) was born and raised in rural Cobden, Illinois, the daughter of the horticulturist and inventor Parker Earle. She received a bachelor of science degree from the University of Illinois in 1885 and subsequently spent several years in the South before moving to New York City. There, she saw her short stories published in the best magazines of the day and also published two novels, *The Wonderful Wheel* (1896) and *The Flag on the Hilltop* (1902). In 1904, she relocated to Cuba where she met her husband, and later moved to California, her home for the rest of her life.

Herbert K. Russell is Director of College Relations at John A. Logan College, Carterville, Illinois. The author of numerous Illinois-oriented writings—bibliographic, biographic, critical, imaginative, and technical—he holds a doctorate in American literature from Southern Illinois University, Carbondale. Recently published writings include an essay on the *Spoon River* poet, Edgar Lee Masters, for the *Dictionary of Literary Biography.* Work in progress includes *Southern Illinois Album, Photos of the Farm Security Administration 1936–1943*, to be published by Southern Illinois University Press. Russell lives in rural Makanda, Illinois, not far from the site of *The Flag on the Hilltop.*

SHAWNEE BOOKS

Also in this series

A Nickel's Worth of Skim Milk
ROBERT J. HASTINGS

A Penny's Worth of Minced Ham
ROBERT J. HASTINGS

Fishing Southern Illinois
ART REID

Foothold on a Hillside
CHARLESS CARAWAY

The Music Came First
THEODORE PASCHEDAG AND THOMAS J. HATTON

Vernacular Architecture in Southern Illinois
JOHN M. COGGESHALL AND JO ANNE NAST

Heartland Blacksmiths
RICHARD REICHELT

The Next New Madrid Earthquake
WILLIAM ATKINSON